But it was better on the floor. There was less smoke. She could breathe a little. And there was someone coming towards her – only a shadow in the smoke, but it was getting nearer. She tried to make a noise, to call out. She hoped that whoever it was could see her. The shadow was getting closer, closer.

And then, with a gasp of horror, Sarah saw the shadow's face: it had long, singed, fair hair and wore a horrible yellow plastic mask. Reaching out for her, the shadowy figure seemed to wear a sickly, terrifying grin. Sarah tried to defend herself, but it was no good – she had no energy left to strike out or run away. He was going to get her.

She passed out.

POINT CRIME

FINAL CUT

David Belbin

Cover illustration by David Wyatt

■SCHOLASTIC

For Mike Russell

Scholastic Children's Books,
Scholastic Publications Ltd,
7–9 Pratt Street, London NW1 0AE, UK

Scholastic Inc.,
555 Broadway, New York, NY 10012-3999, USA

Scholastic Canada Ltd,
123 Newkirk Road, Richmond Hill,
Ontario, Canada L4C 3G5

Ashton Scholastic Pty Ltd,
P O Box 579, Gosford, New South Wales,
Australia

Ashton Scholastic Ltd,
Private Bag 92801, Penrose, Auckland,
New Zealand

First published by Scholastic Publications Ltd, 1994

Text copyright © David Belbin, 1994

Cover illustration copyright © David Wyatt, 1994

ISBN 0 590 55663 0

Typeset by TW Typesetting, Midsomer Norton, Avon
Printed by Cox & Wyman Ltd, Reading, Berks

10 9 8 7 6 5 4 3 2 1

March

Prologue

The moment she walked through the door, every eye in the building turned to Sarah. Someone wolf-whistled. She let herself be ushered to the appropriate place. She was used to attention.

Sarah was nearly six feet tall, and dressed to the nines. She was the model who the Princess of Wales had recently referred to as "breathtaking". She had long, blonde hair and a thin but perfectly proportioned figure. Her face had something harder to define: character, maybe, or charisma, whatever – she didn't know. It was the secret ingredient which people said made her more than very good looking – it made her a great beauty.

Still, Sarah found something unnerving about getting so much attention, here of all places. Then someone said something. The production line started up again. Every eye in the building, including Sarah's, turned to watch it.

From where she was standing, Sarah could see the entire process of assembly. It started at the other end of the factory, with an engine being put onto a conveyor belt. The belt moved on. Robots attached the chassis to the engine: a grey shell, full of gaping holes. At this point, you could hardly tell what it was. Then the body sailed through a shower of red paint and began to resemble what it was to become.

Next, a hundred fans dried the paint. The chassis moved on down the line. Hydraulic arms inserted seats and upholstery. Wheels were added, automatically. Tyres were put on and blown up to the correct pressure. Headlights, tail lights and number plates were fixed in place as the robotic arms scuttled to and fro. Finally, windows were lowered into position, polished and sealed. The completed car was lowered onto the ground and there was a spontaneous round of applause, which Sarah joined in. The whole process had taken barely two minutes.

A man in a white laboratory coat walked up to the car, beaming in the direction of the camera.

"Omega are *proud* to present the *Excelsior*, a car so perfect, so ahead of its time, that the first human hands to touch it could well be *yours*."

There was a noise behind him. One of the car doors – the front passenger one – opened. Sarah gasped. She was seeing something which was impossible, something which made no sense at all. Before her eyes, a young man in jeans and a T-shirt fell out of the car, onto the concrete floor. There was a small red hole in the centre of his forehead, from which blood began to gush. The man's body jerked spasmodically for a second or two, then stopped.

He was dead.

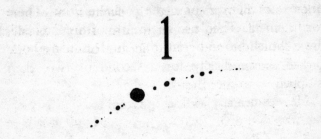

1

"Cut!"

Leo Fitzgerald got down from his director's chair and strolled across to the steadicam operator.

"It looked fine from the monitor. Any problems your end?" The woman shook her head.

Fitzgerald spoke into his megaphone. "All right everybody, that's a take. We're done here."

Suddenly the set, which had been so quiet, sprang into life. At least a hundred people appeared, then vanished almost as quickly. The director walked over to Sarah and extended his hand. Sarah shook it.

"Thanks for fitting me into your schedule. Enjoy the show?" he asked. Sarah grasped for words.

"It was . . . impressive. How did you do that, with the body?" Fitzgerald tapped his nose.

"Professional secret. Maybe when we get to know each other a little better, I'll tell you."

Several people came up to the director, but he motioned them away with the slightest movement of his hand. Then he put his arm around Sarah's bare shoulders, and guided her out of the lot, talking all the time.

"Have you met Brett?"

"No. I'm really looking forward to . . ."

Fitzgerald didn't wait to hear her reply, but kept talking. Like most men, he assumed she was an airhead.

"You might have the look I'm after. How old are you: nineteen? twenty?"

"Seventeen," Sarah admitted.

"You're kidding? You made the cover of *Vogue* at *seventeen*? Way to go! Done any acting?"

Sarah thought about exaggerating her small parts in school plays, then decided against.

"Only a few commercials, when I was younger."

They got into a small buggy, rather like a golf cart, and Fitzgerald began to drive. They crossed the studio complex at a leisurely pace, hardly seeing anybody. It was like being in a ghost town, full of vast, silent warehouses. As he drove, Leo talked. His voice had the usual mid-western lilt, with occasional hints of London.

"There's nothing wrong with doing TV commercials," he told her. "That's where I started. Commercials, rock videos, TV movies – finally a music film, which grossed twenty times what it cost to make. So for the next one – *This Year's Model* – the studio have given me final cut. Know what that means?"

"No."

"It means that what I say goes. When I finish the picture, no one can change a single frame. It means I'm not a hack any longer. I'm an artist. An *auteur*. There aren't many of us left."

"I see."

Sarah wondered if Fitzgerald showed off like this all the time, or was just doing it to impress her. If it was the latter, he needn't have bothered. Since her career had catapulted, barely twelve months ago, Sarah had had every conceivable pick-up technique tried out on her: fashion photographers filled her room with flowers, TV personalities offered her slots in their shows, pop stars promised to produce hit records for her.

So here was a film director, offering to make Sarah a star. She had flown to L.A. today because Sally, her agent, insisted she had to. A major movie would take Sarah right to the top of the supermodel league. But Sarah suspected that Leo Fitzgerald was like all the other men she encountered in the beauty business: sadly shallow.

The director wasn't her type at all. He was thirtyish, with dark, curly hair and a high forehead. He was very thin, and his skin was unnaturally pale for someone who lived in Los Angeles. Sarah was supposed to be flattered when intelligent, mature men were interested in her. She didn't know what she wanted, but it wasn't the men she met. Maybe she needed someone around her own age, someone who didn't make her feel like her teenage years were being snatched away from her.

"Here we are."

They pulled up outside another, newer building. Fitzgerald took Sarah's arm to help her out of the cart, then they walked inside. It was smaller than the huge sound stage she had just left, and so crowded with cameras and sets that it felt claustrophobic.

"What are they making here?" Sarah asked.

"A mini-series. Studios mostly make TV these days. Movies are made on location."

Sarah hadn't realized this. She wondered where *This Year's Model* would be filmed. If the film even existed. Fitzgerald had promised to send Sally a script, but it had never arrived.

"Brett! I hope we haven't kept you waiting."

A tanned, mustachioed actor walked out from between two cameras, smiling over-enthusiastically.

Fleetingly, he looked Sarah up and down, then turned to Fitzgerald. Sarah continued to stare at the actor, remembering all the stories and rumours she'd read about him. The star looked synthetic somehow, as though he'd just stepped out of the screen. Sarah had seen him in a lot of films, and though he hadn't made one for years, he didn't seem to have aged at all.

"She's too young," Johnson told Fitzgerald tersely. "I had my agent check her out. She's seventeen."

"Nearly eighteen," Fitzgerald replied, which wasn't true. "And she looks a lot older. Ask anyone."

"I've got a daughter, twenty-five. How do I look in this picture if I marry a seventeen-year-old?"

Marry? This was the first time Sarah had heard that she was supposed to marry Brett Johnson. She'd thought her role would be a small cameo. According to her agent, Sarah would be playing herself.

"Brett," Fitzgerald coaxed, "believe me: the age gap is sexy. It's dangerous. This is your comeback. You need to reinvent yourself."

Johnson didn't look convinced.

"We've brought her all the way over from England," Fitzgerald went on. "Give the test your best shot."

Johnson nodded. As Fitzgerald told the technicians what to do, the star turned to Sarah and gave her his famous reassuring smile.

"Nothing personal," he said. "Have you read the script?"

"Not yet."

"Don't. It stinks. They're doing a complete re-write on the third act. No one's got any idea how to end the thing."

"Are you ready?" Fitzgerald asked. "I'll go over the lines."

"Do you think that you could tell me the story?" Sarah asked the director. "I was under the impression that this was quite a small role."

"It keeps getting bigger," Fitzgerald told her, with an evasive look. "But basically, it's very simple. The two of you meet, start to fall in love. Brett's a kind of father-figure to you. But he's got a dangerous edge. That's all your character needs to know for this scene. Here. You're Melissa Vine. Brett's Matthew Harper."

Sarah read the page.

INTERIOR. NIGHT. HARPER'S APARTMENT. MATTHEW HANDS MELISSA A COCKTAIL. THEY SIT DOWN ON A SOFA.
HARPER: You were magnificent today.
MELISSA: All I did was dress and undress, pace up and down a catwalk.

HARPER: *Catwalk*. I like that word. It suits you somehow. You're very . . . . feline.

MELISSA LOOKS AWAY: People have warned me about you.

HARPER: But you came back with me anyway. Why?

MELISSA: I don't know. Curiosity, I guess.

HARPER: And we all know what curiosity did to the cat.

THEY KISS.

Sarah put the page down.

"You want us to actually do the kiss?"

"Please. It's important"

She glanced at Johnson. He grinned and pulled a tiny aerosol out of his trouser pocket, then squeezed the breath-freshener into his mouth. Sarah read the script again, not sure if she was meant to learn the lines.

"Let's do it," Fitzgerald said. "And Sarah, don't worry. Just be natural."

Sarah adjusted her make-up, wondering how she was expected to be natural playing a romantic scene opposite a very famous actor who was older than her own father. But she did as she was asked.

She sat on the sofa next to Brett, closer to him than felt comfortable. The lights were very bright and surprisingly hot. Somehow, when she spoke, the words in the script seemed to have etched themselves onto her memory. When Johnson got to the bit about being feline, he began to stroke her neck. His voice purred. Before she knew it, they were kissing. It was a proper kiss, like the ones boys had given her before she was famous. After a few seconds, Johnson pulled away.

"Thank you," Fitzgerald said.

Johnson stood up and offered Sarah his hand.

"Nice meeting you," he said.

Fitzgerald joined him. It seemed to Sarah as though she no longer existed.

"We'll let you know," the director said.

The two men walked out, leaving Sarah alone in front of the bright lights. Sweat ran down her face. She wondered whether she had just been given the Hollywood brush-off. She had been playing it so cool, yet she was aware now that she had taken an important test, and all kinds of things could depend upon it. She felt exposed and very alone.

Then, without warning, the lights went out.

Sarah blinked. The studio was very dark. There were distorted, threatening shadows everywhere. Sarah had no idea how to get out. She shivered. Moments ago it had been stiflingly hot, but now it felt like England in winter. Then she heard a noise, a movement.

"Hello?"

No reply. Sarah began to curse herself. Why

had she come here? She'd just got one career going. She didn't need another one. Before her eyes could adjust to the light, footsteps approached. A silhouette stepped out of the shadows.

"Who?" Sarah stuttered anxiously. "What?"

A hidden hand flicked on a light switch. Standing by the door was a girl, a little older than Sarah.

"Hi. I'm Stacey, Mr Fitzgerald's assistant," she said. "He asked me to drive you back to your hotel."

2

Jonathon Wood often wished that his sister was older than him. Somehow, he felt, it would make things easier. Here he was at eighteen, spending all his time preparing for exams, hoping that he'd got good enough grades to get into university. Meanwhile, seventeen-year-old Sarah was earning thousands and thousands of pounds, travelling all over the world.

It had been this way as long as he could remember. Sarah had started appearing in TV commercials when she was three. After that, she kept getting offers. Things had gone a little quiet between her ninth and thirteenth birthdays – the occasional catalogue job – and Jon thought that she was settling into an ordinary life. His sister even talked about becoming a journalist or something in television.

But then the work picked up, even though she was still at school. It seemed that Sarah's looks (she was the same height as Jon and very thin, with high cheekbones and innocent, enigmatic eyes) were suddenly in fashion. Jon hoped that this fad for child-women would fizzle out, but instead it boomed. In the last year, Sarah Wood had become a household name. Her picture was everywhere.

It even affected his friendships. Jon was never sure whether people really liked him, or were sucking up to him because they wanted a chance to get close to his glamorous sister. He promised himself that when (if) he got to university, he would deny any relationship with Sarah. Wood was a common name, after all. He would make a fresh start.

Jon loved his sister. He didn't envy her, exactly, but he couldn't help resenting her, especially when she rang just after breakfast and told him that she was on the beach at Malibu.

"I thought you were in Paris."

"I *was*. Something came up. That's why I'm ringing. I'm having dinner tonight with this film director, Leo Fitzgerald, and I need some conversation points. Do you know anything about him?"

Jon was a film buff. He spent a lot of his spare time watching videos, or crossing the city on the

Underground, seeking out obscure, crackly prints of minor masterpieces.

"Leo Fitzgerald. Sure. The one who made *Grunge Plunge*?"

"That's right."

"He's a real character. Spent most of his twenties working in a video shop on the King's Road, making rock videos and experimental films in his spare time. He's got this reputation for working really fast and cheap. I think *Grunge Plunge* cost less than a million to make."

"Have you seen it?"

"I saw it at the cinema, yeah. It's a comedy about the Seattle music scene – kind of a beach movie – lots of loud, distorted guitars with indecipherable lyrics. And no story. You'd hate it."

"What else has he done?" Sarah asked.

"I think he did some TV commercials in this country. Then he went to Hollywood, made a couple of TV movies. Do you remember that one about the phantom hitch-hiker and the serial killer? We watched it together at Christmas. That was him."

"Really? It was gruesome."

Jon felt another nugget of information nestling in the back of his mind and tried to dig it out. This was something his friends teased him about: his obsessive appetite for movie trivia.

"Why are you having dinner with him, anyway?" he asked.

"It's a working meal. Sally's coming. I did this audition yesterday. He might have a part in a film for me."

"A part?" Jon laughed incredulously. "I remember you in *Little Red Riding Hood* at primary school. You were dreadful. You're a model, sis, not an actress."

"That was a long time ago," Sarah insisted. "Anyway, thanks for your help. I've got to go. My sunblock's wearing off. If I spend any longer on the beach, I'll start to tan."

As soon as she'd hung up, Jon remembered what he'd read recently about Fitzgerald. It was in the N.M.E.'s movie news section. Fitzgerald was directing a comeback picture for Brett Johnson. The star had won Oscars in the past, but when his career slid, he'd developed a big drink and drugs problem. There'd been a car crash where a passenger was killed. After that, he'd disappeared from view.

Jon wondered why Leo Fitzgerald really wanted to have dinner with his sister. To talk about a part in the film was probably a bluff, he decided. Fitzgerald simply wanted to go out with her, like every other man she met. His sister, an actress? Even she wasn't stupid enough to fall for that one.

"I'm not an actress," Sarah told Fitzgerald, sipping

her Chardonnay and trying to be cool when she was really very excited. "Why me?"

Fitzgerald grinned.

"Why not? Be yourself. This isn't Shakespeare. You're young. You're sexy. You're on the cover of *Vogue*."

Sarah felt out of her depth. She glanced at Sally, who smiled reassuringly.

"I might be comfortable playing myself if this weren't such a big part."

"Other models have gone straight into acting: Lauren Hutton, Brooke Shields, Rene Russo . . ."

"Who?" Sarah wrinkled her nose. These were names she only knew vaguely, names from before she was born. Fitzgerald shrugged.

"I guess they were before your time," he muttered. He leant forward and made intense eye contact.

"Look, if it makes you feel more comfortable, say we're using you for your publicity value. The business these days is all about generating pre-publicity, a buzz. The big movies do most of their business the weekend they open. The hype is everything. You're big news at the moment. The papers are bound to suggest that you're having an affair with the co-star. We'll get lots of mileage out of the denials and no comments."

"Co-star?" Sarah said, trying to hide the distaste in her voice. "You mean Brett?"

"No." Fitzgerald had a twinkle in his eye. "Didn't I tell you? The other major part is Brett's son: Aidan. He falls in love with Melissa and tries to warn her about his father."

"Who plays Aidan?"

"We've only just got him under contract. Luke Kelly."

"*Luke Kelly?*"

Sarah's heart leapt. Luke Kelly was an Irish-American actor with looks to kill for. A year ago, before Sarah's career really took off, he had been her heart-throb. Her wardrobe at home was covered with photographs of the young movie star with deep brown eyes which matched the colour of his long, curly hair.

"That's right. Luke Kelly." Fitzgerald smiled anxiously, uncertain of Sarah's reaction. "Don't believe the stories you've heard about Luke being difficult. He's a pro. And he guarantees millions of extra teenage girls at the box office."

Sarah ate her meal, barely tasting it. Any doubts she had evaporated. She was going to be in a film with Luke Kelly. She must remain cool. Sometimes, it was hard work being sophisticated and successful when you were only seventeen. You couldn't show that anything impressed you. She tried to think of more conversation, but she had already used up all her questions about serial killers and rock videos. Then she thought of one.

"The sequence you were filming today. The dead body in the car. Was it for this film?"

"No," Fitzgerald said. "We're still in pre-production. That was a trailer for a film they're having difficulty promoting. They got me in because it's a bio-flick about a British director."

"So how does the complicated murder fit in with the plot?"

Fitzgerald shrugged. "The plot? Who cares? Like I told you, all that counts in movies these days is getting big numbers at the box office. Ever see *The Big Sleep*? A classic, but the plot had more holes in it than a golf course. You want the plot to make sense? Read a book."

Sarah smiled, not sure if he was joking.

"Where's *This Year's Model* being made?" she asked.

"England. Originally it was going to be New England, but we're on a tight budget and the pound's weak at the moment. So we're filming the entire thing on location in the Home Counties. That's one of the reasons we have to find a British model."

Sarah went to the restroom, in two minds over whether to accept. She'd hoped that she would be working somewhere more exotic than England, where everyone was contemptuous of success and the weather was drab and unreliable. She could think of better places to spend six weeks of the summer. But when she got back to the table, it seemed that a deal had been done. Sally was all enthusiasm, predicting great things for Sarah's future.

"This film will change your life," she told her.

Sarah wondered whether her life hadn't changed enough already. Leo offered his hand. That was the way deals were done in this town. One handshake, and she was committed.

"Are you happy?" he asked, seeing her hesitate.

Sarah thought for a moment, then had an idea. "Could I ask you a favour?"

"Shoot."

"My elder brother, Jon, he's a big movie buff. He's hoping to do Media Studies at university. But he hasn't got a job this summer and he could really use the experience, and some money. Is there any chance you could find him a job on the film?"

Fitzgerald smiled reassuringly. "There are union restrictions, but I'm sure I can work something out."

They shook hands and Sarah's doubts dissolved. It would be good to have her brother along. She hadn't seen enough of Jon in the last year. She didn't want to grow apart from him. And she wanted to share her good fortune. Sarah couldn't believe it. She was going to be in a feature film. She was going to work with Luke Kelly. She could hardly wait.

July

3

The village of Bradlington was small. It was full of old-fashioned shops and chintzy, restored period cottages. The place had a dull, safe air about it which reminded Jon of a hundred other villages his family had driven through on Sunday afternoon outings. He got off the bus at seven in the evening and asked for directions to the hotel.

"There's only one," he was told.

The late Victorian building didn't look big enough to house a whole film crew, but Jon dragged his suitcase into the small lobby.

"I'm with the film," he said at reception.

"What film?"

Half an hour, and an expensive taxi ride later, he found himself at a large, faceless hotel just off a main road, five minutes' drive from Bradlington New Town. Reception told him that his sister hadn't arrived yet. Nor had his room been allocated.

"I've been told to report to the lighting director."

"You'd better wait over there."

Jon sat down on a red sofa, hoping that the evening wasn't going to be an anti-climax. He'd been so excited about the prospect of working on the film this summer that it had been hard to concentrate on his "A" levels. Now they were over, he had no idea how well he had done and, for the moment, he didn't care.

Jon's job, the production assistant explained on the phone, was as a runner, or gofer, as in "go for this, go for that". He should be prepared to do anything, at any time. He sat on the sofa nervously, wondering whether he ought to be seeking out his supervisor. It was late and he was hungry. No one else seemed to be checking in. Maybe he'd made a big mistake by not arriving earlier. This was a cut-throat business; everybody said that. Maybe somebody else had already taken his job. Sarah had assured him that everything was OK, but she'd been out of the country for most of the last four months. They'd hardly spoken.

"Jon?"

A young woman in jeans with closely cropped black hair and a *This Year's Model* T-shirt was standing over him.

"I'm Karen. Nice to meet you."

Jon stood up to shake her hand. Karen's head only came up to his chest.

"Have you eaten?" she asked.

It was hard to tell how old she was – not much more than him. Jon was instantly attracted to her.

"No."

"If I were you, I'd get a sandwich on room service and an early night. You need to be up at five in the morning." She turned to reception and got Jon a key.

"You're sharing with Todd, one of the camera operators."

"Thanks, er . . ."

Jon wondered what Karen's job was: some kind of production assistant, he guessed, but she was not the one he'd spoken to on the phone.

"Actually, I was told to report to the lighting director."

"I know," she said, matter of factly. "That's me."

Jon blushed.

"Get an early night," she told him. "Once this thing gets going, no one'll get much sleep."

But Jon slept badly, too excited to doze off before midnight, when Todd blundered into the room. The shaggy-haired, overweight American had clearly had too much to drink. In the morning, though, he was up first, with no trace of a hangover. He greeted Jon cheerily and regaled him with anecdotes and advice culled from films he'd worked on as they made their way to Bradlington Hall.

By ten, Jon was exhausted and starving. He'd been up since six and he felt like he'd done a full day already. The crew were on a ten-minute break and he was grabbing some coffee and a bacon roll. Karen came into the trailer. Earlier, Ruth Greenwood, the assistant director, had formally introduced them.

"Think of Karen as your adoptive mother," Ruth told Jon.

"Jon, we need some more gaffer tape," his adoptive mother told him now, in a stern voice.

Jon went for it. Todd had warned him – you didn't argue about length of breaks in the movie business. Every second was phenomenally expensive. This was a cheap movie, but the budget was still for several million dollars.

The first scene to be filmed was one where Matthew (Brett Johnson) and Melissa (Sarah) met for the first time. It was an outdoor scene. Melissa was being photographed modelling the English country look. Matthew was staying with the family whose country mansion, Bradlington Hall, provided the backdrop for the shoot. Already, a gaggle of locals had gathered on the edge of the set, watching the crew's preparations.

"Hey, Luke!" someone called.

Jon looked around. A long-haired youth in a parka was pointing towards him.

"That's Luke Kelly," the youth said, and a child standing by him came running over to Jon.

"Luke, Luke, can I have your autograph?"

Jon shook his head.

"I'm not Luke Kelly. He hasn't arrived yet."

The boy looked bitterly disappointed. He walked back towards the onlookers. Jon hurried to Karen with the tape.

"What was that about?" she asked.

Jon shrugged. "Here I am, worried everyone will work out I got the job because I'm Sarah's brother. Instead, people mix me up with Luke Kelly."

Karen examined Jon's looks with an appraising eye. Jon had grown his hair over the summer. Until recently he'd kept it short, and wore glasses a lot, even though he was only a little long-sighted. He didn't like people to comment on his resemblance to Sarah. But all that was about to be changed. He was going to make a new start and wanted a new image to go with it.

Karen's scrutiny embarrassed Jon. She was at least five years older than him, he realized now, and she made him feel like a small boy.

"You do look a little like Luke," Karen said. "Same colour hair. Same build. But your eyes are much kinder than his. I've worked on films with him before. He's . . . in the States, we'd call him a jerk. You know what it means: arrogant, immature, a pain . . . "

"A bit of a prat," Jon translated.

"A prat. Precisely."

"Thanks for the warning," Jon told her, and Karen continued securing the equipment.

It started to rain and everyone retreated to the trailers. Sarah had her own trailer. She had arrived not long before – her flight from the Seychelles had been delayed, and Jon hadn't seen her yet. The crew crammed into the trailer where food was served. The director, Jon was impressed to see, stayed with the crew.

"If this rain doesn't let up," Fitzgerald was saying, "we'll have to move on to the indoor stuff. You'd never think that this was August. Why didn't someone remind me about English summers?"

In a corner of the trailer sat three models, each wearing long, Laura Ashley-style dresses. Why was it that Jon's sister was starring in a film and these women – all older than her – weren't? What did she have that they didn't? Jon expected that they were asking the same question.

The assistant director came into the trailer.

"There's a break in the cloud," Ruth said. "I reckon we've got about ten, fifteen minutes before the skies open up again."

"All right," said Fitzgerald, "let's go for it."

The models were supposed to be being photographed lolling about in front of the mansion. Jon's sister came out of her trailer, long hair flowing around a flimsy, white lace camisole. Beneath it was a long, pleated floral skirt. She walked straight past Jon without acknowledging his presence, taking up her position amongst the models. Jon felt insulted.

"Jon, Leo's monitor needs moving," Karen shouted.

Jon ran for it. There was no time for ego games on a shoot like this, he figured. He'd have time to catch up with his sister later.

Sarah heard someone call her brother's name but she didn't notice him. She was too on edge to take in anything other than the spot where she was meant to be standing. This was an establishing shot of the models on the lawn. For this first scene, Sarah was doing almost exactly what she did every day of her working life – posing.

Chronologically, the scene after this one took place indoors, where Brett Johnson was watching the models. It would be filmed later. For economic reasons, all the scenes in one setting were shot at the same time. So the next to be filmed would be the most important scene, where Matthew and Melissa met for the first time.

The first scene was over before Sarah really

knew it. She began to get nervous. It was easy for Leo to say that all she had to do was play herself. Sarah found it hard enough to be herself when she was with one other person. What did you do when you were surrounded by actors, a crew and cameras which picked up the smallest false note in your performance?

They began the meeting scene. As soon as Brett had been filmed walking over towards Sarah, it started raining again.

"I can't believe it!" Fitzgerald announced over the tannoy. "First day of shooting and we're behind schedule. OK, let's improvise."

Leo called Brett and Sarah over. He began pointing and speaking very quickly. Then it was the technicians' turn. The group came charging back and began rapidly moving equipment in the rain. Sarah saw her brother, but still didn't get a chance to speak to him. He was too busy.

"Don't worry," Brett Johnson said to her, seeming to sense Sarah's unease. "It's always a little crazy on the first day. Everyone will settle down. And you'll be fine. I promise."

"Thank you," Sarah replied. "I hope you're right."

"We're going to do a quick set-up in the summerhouse," Karen explained to Jon. "Melissa will run in there to get out of the rain and Matthew will be waiting for her. It might make a better scene. Come on, give me a hand with this."

Moving the equipment took fifteen minutes. It was a big risk. If the rain stopped, then not only would the move be wasted, but all the equipment would be in the wrong place. But the rain kept coming. The crew didn't have time to secure all the equipment properly. Karen had to stand just off-camera holding a light, so that the actors wouldn't be in shadow. Then, as they were about to start shooting, Leo Fitzgerald had an idea.

"I want to try an overhead shot," he announced.

"We haven't got time to erect scaffolding," Ruth told him.

"Doesn't matter. Quick as you can," he ordered the technicians, "while we're rehearsing the movements. Mount a camera on the tree."

The summerhouse was nearly all glass and an oak tree hung over it.

"I'm not going to sit up there on a branch," the camera operator complained. "Suppose it breaks on me?"

"Just mount the thing somehow," Fitzgerald said. "We'll operate it by remote control."

Jon was summoned to help get the camera up the tree. He carried ladders while other runners brought ropes. Soon they had a pulley in position to lift the camera.

"We should be using scaffolding," the camera

operator complained to Jon. "A more experienced director would know that. But Leo insists on doing everything: director, producer, director of photography . . . he thinks he knows it all, but he doesn't. We'll never get a steady shot with this set-up."

Somehow they got the camera into position, held in place by rope and tape. When it was done, the camera operator refused to climb the tree and crawl along the branch to get the lens pointing in precisely the right direction.

"I'll do it," Jon offered. He was thin and weighed less than ten stone. Heights didn't scare him.

"All right," said Leo. It was the first time he had spoken to Jon. "But be careful. That camera cost a fortune."

Jon climbed five metres up the ladder, then moved across the tree. As children, he and Sarah used to climb trees all the time. It was second nature to him. The branch to which the camera was attached hardly sagged at all. He was sure that it would take his weight easily. But he edged along cautiously, in case the camera wasn't tied on as securely as it should be. The branch moved around a little under his weight, but not much. He felt safe.

The camera wobbled as Jon adjusted its position. Soon, he had it pointing through the appropriate window of the summerhouse. Glancing down the viewfinder, he could see his sister talking to Johnson. Karen's light went on. They had started filming. The image zoomed in. Whoever was operating the remote control focused tightly on Brett and Sarah's faces. Jon's sister was wearing her most childish, innocent expression. Brett reminded Jon of Clark Gable, smiling smugly in *Gone With The Wind*.

The rope attaching the camera to the branch was tight, but Jon put another roll of tape around the camera, just to be on the safe side. Then he inched his way back off the branch. Rain was still pouring heavily. He was soaked through.

"Good job," called the director.

The crew were between takes and Jon headed for the shelter of the summerhouse. Rain pounded onto the glass.

"We're going to do it once more," Fitzgerald announced, "for the overhead shot."

He went over and looked at the monitor, then called to Karen. "You're in shot. Shift to the left a little. Hold the light a bit higher. That's better. Don't move an inch."

Karen, at full stretch, smiled resignedly as Fitzgerald called out, "Action!"

Melissa ran into the summerhouse, almost bumping into Matthew. Her hair, which had been so perfect earlier, was now lank and had darkened with the damp. Her camisole looked like someone had thrown a bucketful of water over it.

"Hello," said Matthew.

"I'm sorry," Melissa responded. "I didn't know there was anybody in here. I'm with . . ."

"Don't apologize," Matthew told her in his honeyed voice. "I came in here to get out of the rain, the same as you. I'm only a visitor here myself. Let me introduce myself. I'm . . ."

Watching them, Jon was surprised by how calm his sister was, how natural. Maybe she *could* act, after all. It annoyed him. Didn't she have enough going for her already?

Fitzgerald didn't make them finish the scene.

"Cut!" he called out. "We've got enough. Let's move into the house."

What happened next seemed to take place in slow motion. The lights went off. Outside, the rain suddenly became even stronger and the summer-house turned darker. Jon felt as though he was under water.

His sister and Brett Johnson started to walk off the set. Behind them, Karen relaxed, put down the light she'd been holding, and followed them. When she reached the precise spot where Jon's sister had been standing a moment before, there was a crashing noise. Shards of glass filled the air. Karen looked up, as did Jon. A huge camera was falling from the broken window, trailing gaffer tape and rope. Karen tried to move, but wasn't quick enough. The camera smashed into her head, knocking the small woman to the ground.

Brett was the first to get to her. Jon wasn't far behind. He looked up at the hole in the ceiling, where rain was beginning to pour through. He thought he saw a shadow moving, but couldn't be sure. Then he turned his attention to Karen.

"How is she?" Jon asked Brett.

The actor shook his head and called to a crew member. "Get an ambulance. And get something to cover her up with."

Sarah came and stood by Jon. It was the first time they'd met in four months, but Sarah said nothing. Members of the crew tried to lift the camera off Karen's body. Brett stood up and turned to Sarah.

"Don't look," he said. "The camera smashed her face in. It's not a pretty sight."

Sarah turned to Jon.

"That could have been me," she told him.

Immediately, people surrounded Sarah, comforting her. Jon edged away. It was as though Sarah was the one who had died, not Karen. The lighting director's lifeless body lay sprawled across the summerhouse floor. Jon stared at it in horror. He'd never seen a dead person before. Karen's face was turned away from him. She didn't look dead at all. She looked like she would get up at any moment and tease him for being so worried, then order him to put the broken camera away.

Jon left his sister with Brett Johnson and the others, and ran outside into the heavy rain. Had there been someone in the tree? If there had been, there wasn't now. There were no longer any bystanders either, though there had been a dozen watching the filming earlier. Everyone but Jon was under cover. He stayed out in the rain, trying to take in what had happened. Only minutes before, Karen had been flirting with him. Now she was dead. How could life end so quickly, so meaninglessly? Jon stood by the tree as water splashed down his face, watching shadows in the rain.

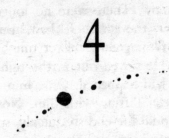

4

"**Y**ou can't blame yourself," Sarah told Jon. They were sitting together in her trailer, waiting for the police. It wasn't a joyous reunion. Sarah had apologized for not greeting him earlier. There hadn't been a spare moment, she said.

"I feel responsible," Jon told her.

"It wasn't your job to attach the camera to the tree."

"But I was up there."

"Yes, and you put some extra tape on to secure it. I watched you. If it hadn't been for that, the thing might have given way before. Ten seconds earlier and that camera would have landed directly on me!"

"There's something else," Jon told her. "I

thought I saw someone, or something, up there in the tree."

Sarah frowned. "It must have been your imagination."

Jon shook his head.

"Or a squirrel," Sarah said.

"That camera was secure. I know," Jon insisted.

"That camera weighed half a tonne. And the rain suddenly got heavier. The weight was too much. It was an accident."

"I'm not sure."

They were joined by Leo Fitzgerald, who looked unnaturally calm. He spoke to Jon.

"The police are on their way. Please don't blame yourself in any way. It was a tragic, freak accident. If anyone's to blame, it was me. We should have used scaffolding." He turned to Sarah. "We're going to suspend filming for a while. I'll get someone to drive you back to the hotel."

"Do you want me to stay with you?" Sarah asked her brother.

"No. I'll be OK."

While he was waiting for the police, Jon walked over to the camera in the summerhouse. Karen's body had been taken away by the ambulance workers, but there was a tiny patch of blood on the floor by the camera. Jon looked at the black masking tape, trying to work out where it had split, and why. Despite what his sister had said, the camera didn't weigh that much, probably less than he did.

And then there was the rope . . . it hadn't torn, as you would have expected, but seemed to have unravelled. Yet Jon was sure that the knots had been tight. He'd had trouble moving the camera around. Had he loosened them somehow? Was Karen's death his fault? What if her death wasn't an accident? No, that was absurd. What else could it be?

"Mr Wood?"

"Yes."

"Detective Sergeant Wilson. Can I have a word?"

Jon answered the policewoman's questions about what had happened. At first the questions were gentle, but as they went on, the interview turned into a grilling.

"Are you trained in safety procedures for such circumstances?"

"No."

"What qualifications did you have for operating the camera?"

"None. But I wasn't operating it, I was securing it. They asked me to do it because I'm light and good at climbing trees."

"'Good at climbing trees'," the sergeant said aloud as she wrote it down in her notebook. "I'm sure that will impress the jury at the inquest."

"But look," Jon said, "I'm not sure that the camera falling *was* an accident. I thought I saw someone moving in the tree just after it fell. And if you examine the way the tape's been torn . . ."

"That's enough," the policewoman said, like a teacher silencing an impertinent pupil. Jon shut up.

"Listen," the sergeant went on, more kindly. "I expect you blame yourself for what happened. You shouldn't. I blame the people who were supposed to be in charge. But don't start making up stories about sabotage. The dead woman has a family. Silly stories at the inquest would upset them. Do you follow me?"

"Yes," said Jon. "But the tape . . ."

"Forensic will look at it. You can go now."

Jon slunk away. Most of the crew had gone back to the hotel. He should join them there and await instructions, but he didn't feel like being around film people at the moment. He felt like being alone. The rain was easing off. He walked towards the woodland on the edge of the estate.

"Hey!"

He had bumped into a figure in a hooded anorak, coming out of the woods. "Sorry," he told the youth. "I was miles away."

The youth gave him a sullen look.

"I saw you earlier. You're not Luke Kelly, are you?"

Jon shook his head.

"You look like him."

"If you say so."

The youth removed his hood. He had long, straggly, fair hair and a pallid, spotty face.

"You're working on the film though?"

"That's right."

"What was that big crash an hour ago? I was sheltering from the rain. When I came out of the woods an ambulance was leaving and the police were arriving."

"There was an accident. A camera fell on someone and she got killed."

"She?"

"One of the crew."

The youth shook his head. "Bummer! That's why everyone's leaving, huh?"

"That's right."

"Dangerous business, the movies. Look, I hope you don't mind me asking, but, like, is there any chance of me getting a job on the film? Extra, runner, cook – I'd do anything. What did this woman do?"

Jon shrugged. Karen had been dead less than an hour and already someone was trying to get her job.

"I'm not the one to ask," he told the youth. "It's my first day in the business. I'm the lowest of the low."

"How did you get your job?" the youth asked.

Jon evaded answering precisely. "Favour from a friend."

The boy nodded. "Connections. It's all about connections." He started to walk away. "Thanks anyway."

"Hold on," said Jon, not sure whether to be suspicious of the guy or sorry for him. "What's your name? If I hear anything . . ."

"People call me 'Slacker'," the youth said. "Call me that if you like."

"And where do you live?"

"I'll be around," Slacker told him. "You'll see me."

"I'll see you around, then. My name's Jon."

"See you, Jon."

That guy could be me, Jon thought as he walked away. Nothing to do all summer, hanging around pathetically for a taste of the action. Maybe Jon would be able to put in a word for Slacker. That was if he still had a job himself, after what had happened today.

By the next day, at the hotel, nobody was discussing the accident, as though talking about it might bring on further bad luck. Karen's body would be flown home, Jon learned. A replacement for her had been hired already. The studio would probably be fined for breaking safety procedures. Karen's family would get an out-of-court settlement.

It seemed that Slacker was right: this sort of thing happened all the time.

Jon went to the bar. There, all the talk centred on Luke Kelly. The teen idol was due to arrive the next day. He wouldn't be on location for the whole shoot, as he was booked to star in another movie in five weeks' time.

"What's he like?" Jon asked Todd, his room mate, remembering what Karen had told him earlier.

Todd grinned salaciously. "Luke likes to party, in every sense of the word. But he's not . . . you know, one of those brat-pack types. He's a loner. Never keeps a girlfriend longer than it takes to make a picture. Doesn't have any friends outside the business. He's a little weird, I guess, but a lot of people get that way when they make it early."

Jon nodded, thinking about his sister. How was she handling fame? He'd seen so little of her over the last year that it was hard to be sure.

"How old is Kelly?" he asked.

"Twenty-two, three, something like that. Made his first film five years ago, playing one of the Beach Boys. *Surf's Up*. See it?"

Jon shook his head.

"Lousy movie. Even the cover versions of the songs were dreadful. But Luke took his shirt off a lot, and it was a hit with teenage girls. He got the lead role in the first *Cool College* feature and he had it made. He's been taking his shirt off ever since."

Jon laughed.

"There is one thing about Luke," Todd went on. "He's big on practical jokes. You wake up in the morning and there's a horse's head on your pillow, or you get in your car and find someone's filled it with sand, that'll be Luke."

"He sounds like a fun kind of guy," Jon said sarcastically.

Todd looked like he was going to say something, then glanced downwards instead. One of the other actors must have come into the room. You didn't badmouth actors in front of their colleagues – that was something which Jon had already learned. All actors were notoriously insecure, and would assume that you were saying similar things about them. Jon turned round to see who had walked into the room.

"Hi," said his sister.

"Hi," Jon mumbled.

Sarah was wearing jeans and a T-shirt. She looked like a normal person for once. Some of the colour had returned to her face since the day before. They gave each other a hug.

"You eaten yet?" Sarah asked him.

"Not hungry."

"Come to the restaurant with me. I could use some company."

Jon gave Todd a reluctant shrug, and joined

Sarah. He could hardly not go with his sister. She had got him the job, after all, and the accident yesterday must have been as big a shock for her as it was for him. But he couldn't help resenting the way she had asked him.

Several of the other actors and the director were in the restaurant. There was a kind of pecking order, Jon realized. The talent ate first. The crew came later. He shouldn't be here.

Fitzgerald nodded at Sarah.

"Chef tells me the chicken's very good," he said.

"Maybe," Sarah said, "but I'm a vegetarian."

They sat at a table on their own. Jon ordered the chicken, Sarah asked for stuffed peppers.

"What have you been doing?" she asked him.

He told her about the set he'd been working on at Bradlington Hall.

"How about you?" he asked when he'd finished.

"I've been reading the script, or what they've given me of it. They won't explain the ending – Leo says they've got someone in Hollywood working on a re-write."

"What's the script like?"

Sarah shrugged. "I'm no judge. I've never read one before. Come up to my room later. I'd like your opinion."

"In other words," Jon said, "you don't like it."

"There are one or two things I'm not . . ."

She looked up. Three waiters were bringing in

large silver salvers, which had covers on to keep the chicken hot. Ceremoniously, they deposited each of the salvers on the film entourage's tables at precisely the same moment. Jon hadn't realized that this was so posh a hotel. From the kitchen came a loud, stagey voice, speaking in a mock English accent.

"Dinner is served."

On the last word, each of the waiters whipped off the covers to the salvers. Three chickens began to hurtle across the tables, their feathers flying everywhere. Blood spattered the tablecloth. Jon saw that the chickens' heads had been cut off.

Someone screamed. Sarah flinched and grabbed Jon's arm in shock. He looked around. In the entrance to the dining area, various members of the crew were looking on, laughing hysterically.

The chickens were dead within seconds.

"Who's that?" Sarah asked.

A man in a white coat and a huge chef's hat came out of the kitchen, grinning demoniacally. When he whipped the hat off his head, Jon recognized him at once. It was Luke Kelly.

5

Sarah recognized the film star when he took his hat off. She felt sickened, humiliated. There was blood on her T-shirt. Across the table from her, Jon looked angry. At the entrance to the dining room, members of the crew were laughing, as though this was a huge joke. The director and the people sitting around him started to laugh awkwardly too. They didn't want to offend the big American star. Only Brett Johnson remained stony-faced. Jon stood up, his face brittle with anger.

"Let's go and eat somewhere else."

Sarah pulled her brother back towards his seat.

"No, we'd better stay. I've got to work with him, even if he is a jerk. Would you hold our table while I change my T-shirt?"

Jon nodded, sitting down reluctantly. Sarah had to walk past Kelly and the crew to get upstairs. She avoided looking at the American actor.

"Hey!"

Luke Kelly grabbed Sarah by the forearm as she passed him. She turned to face him. In the flesh he was even better looking than on the pictures she'd pinned to her wardrobe door. Somehow, this made her feel even angrier.

"Let go of me!"

Kelly smirked his famous smirk.

"A woman with a temper. I like that. Leo tells me that we're going to fall in love."

Sarah almost blushed. For the last four months, she'd been having daydreams about Luke Kelly. In them, he would ask her out while they were making the film. Had Fitzgerald somehow guessed this?

"Pardon?" she said to the actor.

"We fall in love in the movie. I steal you from my daddy."

"Is that right?" Sarah snapped. "I haven't got that far in my copy of the script. I'll take a look at it now, when I'm upstairs, getting rid of my blood-stained clothes."

Kelly looked a little sheepish.

"Sorry about that. I didn't mean to make you scream, either. It was just my little way of intro-ducing myself."

"It was infantile," Sarah told him. "And cruel. Oh, and that wasn't me screaming. It was one of the waitresses. If you're so sorry about it, why don't you go over and apologize to her?"

"Calm down, Sarah," Leo said. "It was only a little joke."

"No," said Kelly. "She's right." He got up and walked over to the waitress, who was busy removing chicken feathers from the floor.

Sarah didn't watch any further. She went up to her room. Maybe she'd order some dinner on room service, read the rest of the script there. She felt dirty, defiled. She needed a shower.

In her room, Sarah undressed, throwing the cotton T-shirt into a bin. It wasn't worth saving. The blood would never come out properly. In the shower booth, she turned the water onto hot, then tucked her hair into a shower cap and increased the pressure so that it pounded her body. Maybe she wouldn't eat at all. She'd have an early night. She had to be on set at six in the morning.

The shower refreshed her. She'd get that script read before she went to bed. She turned off the water, and was about to get out of the booth when she thought she heard a noise. She listened carefully. Water still dripped from the shower nozzle, but she heard what sounded like a door opening and closing. Then there was a voice. Sarah couldn't distinguish the words. It must be next door, she told herself. She was nervous for no reason. Pulling the shower curtain aside, she reached for her towel. Then she heard footsteps.

Sarah stepped back into the shower booth and pulled the curtain to, concealing herself. Who was in her room? What did they want? She stood stock still in the shower, hoping that whoever it was would go away. She felt rattled. The lighting director's death had unsettled her. Jon's suggestion that it wasn't an accident was even more unnerving. What if . . . ? But no, that was too preposterous.

Who was at the door? It couldn't be the maid, not at this time of the evening. Suppose it was Luke Kelly, playing another practical joke? The footsteps were coming towards her. Someone was calling her name, but she couldn't hear the voice properly because of the dripping shower nozzle.

"Sarah?"

If it was Kelly, she wanted a towel around her. Sarah told herself not to be nervous. She wasn't in any danger here, not in a hotel in the Home Counties. She pushed the shower curtain aside and reached to the rail for the large white bath towel that was hanging there.

"Sis!"

Sarah jumped as her brother poked his head into the bathroom.

"There you are. I was worried about you. You said you'd come straight back down."

Sarah stepped out of the shower, relieved.

"I'm sorry," she said. "I forgot. I just . . ."

Jon began to laugh.

"You're white as a sheet," he said, "and you look really silly in that shower cap."

Sarah laughed too.

"Let's get some supper on room service," she said. "And we can look at the script together. Is that OK?"

"Fine by me," Jon said. "The atmosphere in that dining room's turned poisonous."

Sarah dressed in the bathroom while Jonathon ordered food. Then he kicked off his shoes and they sat on the bed reading the loose pages of the script. Sarah picked up from where she had left off earlier. The script wasn't complete, but there was enough of it for her to see that Luke Kelly had been telling the truth. She had two passionate love scenes with him. Now that she'd found out he was so obnoxious, how was she going to handle them?

When Jon got to the love scene pages, he burst out laughing. "I see you get to undress Luke Kelly. That should be fun."

Sarah frowned. "He's the one with the sense of humour."

"You used to like him," Jon said. "Didn't you?"

Sarah cringed. There were some things you didn't need an older brother around to remind you about.

"You won't tell anyone, will you?"

"Now would I do a thing like that?" Jon replied, teasing her.

Sarah thumped her brother with a pillow.

"You'd better not, or I'll . . . I'll . . ."

Jon grabbed the other pillow and held it over her head. "You'll what?"

As they swung pillows at each other there was a knock on the door. Sarah burst into a fit of giggling. There was another knock.

"Yes?" Jon said, finally recovering himself.

"Room service."

They kept reading as they ate their food, getting the script greasy.

"What do you think?" Sarah asked, when her brother had got to the last page.

Jon was diplomatic.

"You've certainly got a big part. Are they paying you enough?"

"My agent will sort that out. What do you think of the story?"

Jon shrugged. "It reminds me of that old Hitchcock movie, *Suspicion*, with Brett Johnson in the role that Cary Grant played. Is he a wife-killer, or is he perfectly innocent? You're never sure if the wife's in danger or not. In this screenplay, the writer doesn't seem to have made up his mind."

"Was Cary Grant guilty in the end?" Sarah asked.

Jon shook his head. "Hitchcock meant him to be, but the studio made him go for a typical Hollywood compromise ending. Anyhow, the twist in this script is the Luke Kelly character. Is he what his father says he is: a no-good, scrounging waster? Or does he really have the lowdown on the father, who marries models then murders them? I think the current ending's a bit weak."

"Maybe you think they should make me into the villain?"

"Interesting idea," Jon said, "but I don't think it'd fit. Anyway, the film's got to finish with you in the arms of the hero."

"That's a relief," Sarah said. "At least you don't think that I'm going to get killed."

Jon smiled. "You're kidding. How many films have you seen? They never kill the beautiful girl. She's got to kiss the hero in the final scene."

Sarah looked at her watch. It was nearly ten.

"We'd better get to bed. Early start in the morning."

Jon nodded. "I have to be on set an hour before you do."

He paused, deciding whether to say something.

"You know, I thought – from what I saw before

the accident – you were good today. I was impressed."

Sarah was impressed too. She couldn't remember the last time her brother had praised her.

"Thanks," she said. "That means a lot to me. G'night."

"G'night."

A moment after he had gone, there was a knock on the door. Sarah noticed that her brother's trainers were still on the floor. He might be able to walk around the hotel barefoot, but he'd need them in the morning.

"Come in, stupid!"

The door opened.

"How did you know I was stupid?"

Sarah looked up to see the grinning face of Luke Kelly.

"What do you want?" she snapped.

"Aw, come on," Kelly gave her his famous "who, me?" smile. "Please don't bite my head off. I came to apologize. I was waiting for you to come back downstairs. Then, when you didn't, I found out which room was yours. I've been standing round the corner. I didn't want to embarrass you by walking in on you and your boyfriend."

"Who told you that he's my boyfriend? He's . . ."

Kelly grinned. Already, she realized with irritation, he had her on the defensive.

"Hey," he said, "I don't want to pry into your private life. Who you hang around with is your concern. Right?"

"Right."

Let him think that Jon's my boyfriend, Sarah decided. What does it matter?

"But I hope we can be friends," Luke went on. "We got off on the wrong foot. I'm sorry."

He offered her his hand, smiling sheepishly. "Apology accepted?"

"Apology accepted, I guess."

His hands were surprisingly soft and warm. There was a twinkle in his eyes as he said goodnight. He's awfully good-looking, Sarah thought, as she shut the door on him, and locked it; but he's far too fond of himself for his own good.

She got into bed, but, although she was tired, found it hard to sleep. Her mind kept going over the last two tumultuous days. One thought stuck with her. Suppose Jon's earlier suspicions were right? Suppose the lighting director's death wasn't an accident?

When she finally slept, Sarah's dreams were filled with odd images. Grinning gargoyles in chef's hats fell from trees. Then, before they could hit the ground, the gargoyles turned into smiling, seductive film stars. At one point she dreamt that she woke, and that somebody was in the room with her. Each dream was punctuated by a dead, dark-haired body, sometimes on the summerhouse floor, sometimes falling from a car. And all the while, in every dream, Sarah had the sense that she was being watched. But why, and by whom, she couldn't say.

6

Melissa gazed into Matthew's eyes. They had just spent a wonderful afternoon together, boating on the lake. But now it was time for her to go.

"I love you," Matthew said. "Don't leave me."

Melissa stroked his hand.

"You're a wonderful man, but I've only known you for a few days. You've got a past that I know nothing about. And you're so much older than I am."

"None of that counts. All that matters is the future, *our* future. I can make you happy, Melissa. No one else can make you as happy as I can. If you think I'm wrong, tell me."

He was holding her tightly now. The script

called for him to get back in the boat in a moment. But they were in the wrong positions. Sarah tried not to think about this as she said her lines.

"I think I love you, Matthew. But I'm scared . . ."

"Don't be scared, my darling. Be brave. Marry me."

"Oh, Matthew . . ."

The actor relinquished her now and took a step backwards.

"Don't answer me now. I'll come back tonight. Tell me your decision the—"

As he was speaking, Brett took another step backwards and lost his footing. He slid, landing on his bottom in the motorboat.

"Cut!"

Everybody was laughing, except Brett.

"Are you all right?" Sarah asked, getting into the boat with him. "That was a nasty fall."

Brett sat up. "I think only my dignity is hurt." He called to the director. "What went wrong there?"

"You got carried away," Fitzgerald called. "Moved out of position. We'll rehearse it again before the next take. Do you remember how to start the boat?"

"Good question," Brett replied. He smiled at Sarah. "I'm not the world's most practical man."

He reached for the cord coming out of the engine. "I pull this, don't I?"

"That's right."

Brett pulled it, and the engine roared into life.

"At least it works," Brett said. The boat pulled away from the quay.

"How do I stop it?" Brett called over the engine noise, as the boat strained the rope holding it.

"Try pulling the cord again."

Brett did, but the cord gave way in his hands. The actor cursed. As he spoke, the small speedboat snapped its line to the quay, and hurtled off into the lake. Brett swore again.

"Any idea how to steer this thing?" he asked Sarah, who was sitting at the end farthest from the engine. As the boat picked up speed, Sarah shook her head and clambered towards him. Brett reached for the steering wheel. Sarah tried to stay calm, but the boat was going faster still. She had to work out how to switch the engine off.

On the quay, members of the crew began gesticulating at them. Then Sarah saw the reason why. Blue flames were starting to streak around the engine. Black smoke poured into the air as the flames grew bigger. They were on fire. Sarah turned to Brett.

"Jump off!" she called.

"I can't."

"We're on fire. You have to."

"I can't. I'm afraid of water. I can't swim!"

Sarah pulled out the one lifejacket attached to

the deck. "Then take this, before it's too late. Now!"

Brett let Sarah put the yellow jacket round his neck. Then, quickly, without looking back, she dived into the water.

The lake was dirty and deep. As Sarah surfaced, several metres away from the boat, she heard an enormous bang. Looking over, as her eyes cleared, she saw that the engine had exploded. The whole boat was aflame. Noxious, oily smoke drifted over to her, making it difficult to breathe. She dipped underwater again, trying to swim back towards the quay, hoping that Brett had jumped off in time.

Sarah surfaced again, unable to see Brett or the shore through the smoke. Did the crew have a lifeboat? She had no idea. She went under once more in order to avoid the smoke which was starting to suffocate her. Her clothes were too heavy. They were dragging her down. She managed to kick off her shoes, then swam away from the smoke, surfacing again in cleaner air. She took a few gulps of air and looked around. She still couldn't see the shore.

It amazed her that Brett couldn't swim. But Sarah wasn't that good a swimmer herself. A handful of lengths was usually her limit, and she didn't like to linger in the deep end. What made it worse now was that she didn't know in which direction she was going. The quay could be anywhere.

Maybe it was hidden by the smoke. She could see some green land, a hundred metres or so away. It could be the shore, or it could be the little island in the middle of the lake. Either way, she would be safe there. Sarah swam towards it.

A hundred metres wasn't far. But in cold, clammy water, with a soaked summer dress, she couldn't move quickly. And the smoke from the burning engine must have got into her lungs, too. She was finding it hard to breathe properly. Where was everybody? She was getting nearer to land. She could make out detail. But she was slowing down. She could see grass, trees. There was someone standing in the trees, watching her. Why didn't he come and help her? Sarah's legs were tired. She couldn't go much further. And her head ached. How it ached!

She relaxed for a moment and took in a mouthful of water. Summoning all her strength, she lifted her head up and spluttered the water out. But then she was coughing and going under again. It wasn't fair. She was so close. It wasn't . . .

"Here. Grab on to me."

Strong arms reached around her shoulders.

"Just let your body relax. Let me swim you to the shore."

Sarah felt herself moving more quickly. Then she began to lose consciousness.

"Don't pass out," said the familiar, reassuring

voice. "You've got to keep breathing. It's not far now."

Somehow, Sarah managed to keep her head above water.

The next thing she knew, she was on dry land, being given mouth-to-mouth resuscitation by the crew nurse. Her body convulsed for a moment, then she vomited up the rest of the putrid water she had swallowed.

"She'll be all right now," Sarah heard the nurse saying. Then her brother was standing over her.

"How do you feel?" he asked, tenderly.

"I'll live. How's Brett?"

"They're just bringing him in now. But he'll be all right. He had a lifejacket on but you had to swim all that way. You nearly made it."

"Was it you," Sarah asked, gratefully, "who brought me in?"

Jon shook his head.

"I wasn't here. They sent to the house for me. It was him." He pointed to the figure sitting on the lawn in wet boxer shorts, talking to the director. Sarah's heart pounded heavily. Her life had been saved by Luke Kelly.

"Come on," said the nurse. "We're going to get you back to the hotel and into a hot shower and a warm bed for a while."

"I need to thank . . ."

"You can do that later. Help me with her, would you, Jon?"

Jon and the nurse lifted her into a waiting land-rover. Her brother offered to go with her but Sarah refused.

"Speak to Luke for me, would you?" she asked him. "Say . . ."

"I know what to say. Take care of yourself."

"OK."

The landrover started off, then slowed down again by the quay. The nurse got out and returned with Brett Johnson. He looked pale.

"You showed great presence of mind there," he told Sarah. "If you hadn't put that lifejacket on me, I might . . ."

"Don't be silly," Sarah told him. "But I'm sur-prised at a big grown man like you, never learning to swim."

"It's a phobia," Brett told her. "My shrink reckons I must have been thrown into deep water somewhere when I was a child, and never recovered. She can't cure me of it. I used to keep it secret, but the scandal sheets 'exposed my weakness' when they were dumping on me a few years back."

"That's a nasty thing to do," Sarah told him, sleepily. Then her head became woozy again and she passed out.

When his sister had gone, Jon walked over to the

young American. Someone had given Luke a towel and he was drying himself off.

"Sarah asked me to thank you for what you did."

Kelly nodded brusquely. "It was nothing. Anybody would have done it. I just happened to be nearest."

A girl from Costume came over. "We've got some substitute clothes lined up. If you'd like to come to the trailer . . ."

"In a minute." He smiled at Jon. "The show goes on. They're going to film my first scene. I stand by the shore, watching my father, jealous of his lusty young fiancée. Why did I agree to do this junk?"

Jon felt no need to be diplomatic. "Because it's got more class than *Cool College 5*?"

Luke raised his hands in mock surrender. "True, that's the film I'm making next. But the only class in this film comes from your girlfriend."

"Girlfriend?" Jon asked, awkwardly. "You mean Sarah?"

"You're a lucky guy. She's something special."

"That's as may be, but she's not my girlfriend."

"Oh, come on," said Luke, with a glint in his eye. "What were you doing in her room late last night? Why did Leo send for you when she nearly drowned?"

"Because," Jon explained slowly, "she's my sister."

Luke blinked. "You're kidding?" he said. He looked closely at Jon's face. "No, I can see you're not."

"You're right. I'm not."

Kelly smiled. "In that case," he said, "I hope the two of us can be friends."

He offered Jon his hand. Jon was reluctant to take it but, after all, Kelly had just saved his sister's life . . . maybe. They shook hands.

"Gotta go," Luke told him. "Clothes to wear, scenes to shoot. Maybe we can have a drink together in the bar tonight."

"Yes," said Jon. "Maybe."

When Luke had gone, Jon tried to work out what Luke meant when he said "in that case". He thought he knew. Luke had planned to take Jon's girlfriend away from him. Now that he knew she wasn't his girlfriend, the two of them could be friends. If that was the way Hollywood stars acted, Jon wanted no part of it.

Jon walked back towards the lake where the remains of the boat had been dragged onto the shore. As he turned out of sight of the crew, a familiar long-haired figure came out of the woodland.

"Hi, Jon! How are you?"

"I'm OK," Jon replied, reluctant to call the youth Slacker, which he thought was a stupid name. "But

I haven't had an opportunity to ask about a job for you. There's been too much going on."

"That's all right," Slacker said. "I know it's a long shot. Was that Luke Kelly I saw you talking to just now?"

"That's right," said Jon, wondering why the youth was so interested in Kelly.

"What's he like?"

"About as funny as a headless chicken," Jon replied, listlessly.

Slacker looked confused. "People say he's a bit of a brat. How's he getting on with Brett Johnson?"

"I wouldn't know," Jon replied.

He was suddenly suspicious. Suppose Slacker was a stringer for one of the newspapers? He seemed very inquisitive, for a fan. The crew were under strict instructions not to let out any gossip from the set.

"Why do you hang around here all the time?" Jon asked the youth.

"I'm just after a job, like yours, you know? I'm on the dole. I'd like to get into a film school, but I haven't got the qualifications. If I could get some experience . . ."

"If I were you," Jonn said, in a cordial but distanced voice, "I'd try and talk to the casting director or the location manager."

"I'd be willing to work for free . . ."

"The most they can do is say 'no'," Jon told him.

"Everyone'll be moving over to the house after they shoot a short scene with Luke in it. Maybe you can catch them then."

"Thanks," said the youth. "I appreciate it."

"You're welcome."

When Slacker had gone, Jon examined the boat. What remained of the engine was a charred ruin. The hulk of the boat was intact, but badly burnt. Could someone have sabotaged it in some way? There was no way for Jon to tell. One accident proved nothing. Even two could still be a coincidence. A third would prove sabotage. But what happened if the culprit was third time lucky?

Back at the hotel, Sarah collapsed onto her bed.

"Just an accident," Leo had insisted. "There was no real danger."

Not to Brett, perhaps, in his lifejacket, but she had never felt more scared. Sarah resolved not to put herself near any risky situations for the rest of the film.

Although she felt knocked out by her ordeal, she couldn't sleep. Finally, she sat up. She would read the script again, making sure that she could insist on safety precautions for every possibility. There was a fire scene, for instance: she wanted lots of extinguishers, a doctor – you name it. And she'd better ask about the ending. If there was going to be some kind of chase across the roof of Bradlington Hall, as Leo was considering, then she wanted a stunt double.

Sarah leant down to pick up her script where she'd left it that morning, beside the bed. It wasn't there. She felt under the bed. Nothing but the sneakers Jon had left the night before. Where was the script? She must have taken it with her this morning. But no, she had learnt her lines. There'd been no need. Maybe a maid had been in, tidied it away. Sarah was too tired to get up and look for it now. Anyway, who would want a script? It had no financial value.

Suddenly, she felt very tired. She'd find the script when she woke up. And, if she'd mislaid it, she could always get another one. Her mind drifted off into shallow, dreamless sleep.

7

Film-making, Jon decided, was another world, where the normal rules no longer applied. Whatever disasters occurred, however little sleep you got, the demands of the moment swept you along. When Sarah and Brett returned to the set the next day, both looking only a little the worse for wear, there was a spontaneous round of applause from the crew and the rest of the cast. But then it was straight into work. They were filming the ballroom scene.

Extras flooded the house. Jon noticed Slacker, with his hair tied back, dressed as a waiter. He must have talked his way into a job, after Jon's advice that morning. That was good, because it would get him off Jon's back. Slacker couldn't be in Equity, the actors' union, but then, neither was Jon. Leo bent rules, or simply ignored them, all the time. He was short of extras, so everyone pitched in.

Jon was dressed in a tuxedo, the first time he'd ever worn one, and paired with a glamorous girl who had played one of the models the day before.

"How many movies have you been in?" she asked.

"None. This is the first."

"Mine too. I'm Mary."

"Jon."

"You must have done some acting . . . on the stage?"

Jon shook his head. "I'm not an actor. I'm just a . . . general dogsbody. I'm doing this for the experience, before I go to university."

"Film school?"

"Hardly. Media Studies and Humanities. How about you?"

"I get by," Mary said, casually. "I had a walk-on in *Casualty* recently. I've got some auditions coming up." She glanced over Jon's shoulder. "You know what makes me really sick?"

"What?"

"People like her." Mary pointed at Jon's sister. "She's got a career already, modelling. Fitzgerald has half a dozen hot actresses audition for the role, then goes and hires some tramp who's never acted in her life. I'll bet they're an item."

"I don't think so," said Jon, diplomatically. "Maybe she got lucky. It's the way of the world – those who have, get more."

"Isn't it just!"

"Action!" the director called.

Matthew and Melissa were in the middle of the ballroom, dancing, when suddenly Matthew stopped.

"What is it?" Melissa asked, concerned.

"Somebody I didn't expect to see."

"You want to leave?"

Slowly, Matthew shook his head. "It's all right. He's seen us now."

The steadicam tracked Aidan, walking across the crowded dance floor towards Melissa and Matthew. Aidan's face was sombre, emotionless. The two men faced up to each other in silence. Finally, as the music ended, Matthew spoke.

"Melissa, this is my son, Aidan."

"Your *son*?"

"Aidan, this is my fiancée, Melissa."

"*Fiancée*? Again?"

Melissa gave a small start when Aidan said the word *again*. Jon's sister and Luke Kelly looked at each other with their eyes on fire. Was that acting, Jon wondered? Or was it a result of what had happened the day before, when Luke rescued Sarah?

"Perhaps," Aidan said, "I could have this dance with my stepmother-to-be?"

The band struck up a waltz. Matthew held on to Melissa.

"Not today, Aidan. Maybe at the wedding . . . *if* you're invited." Aidan bowed curtly and walked off, straight in front of Jon and Mary.

"Cut!"

"Oh, that was brilliant!" said Mary.

"Did you think so?" Jon asked her. He'd thought Sarah's acting was OK, but not brilliant.

"Yes. The way he walked past us. There's no way they can cut us out of that scene now. We're bound to be in the finished film."

The extras were moved away while Fitzgerald shot the next scene, where Matthew and Melissa had their first argument. Jon watched as his sister did a convincing job of losing her temper.

"Is there anything else you're keeping from me? Are you sure that you don't have any *grandchildren* I should know about?"

"Aidan's my only child."

"What did he mean when he said *again*? How many times have you been married?"

"I don't like to talk about my marriages."

"Why not? I love you, Matthew. But we can't make a life together if you keep secrets from me."

"I promise, darling. I'll tell you everything, in time."

"I'm not sure if I can wait that long."

Melissa, her eyes artificially watering with nitro-glycerine, walked away.

Sarah was exhilarated. She hadn't realized how much fun acting would be, compared to modelling. Some things were the same: the waiting around; the constant attention; the endless make-up and wardrobe sessions. Preparation took up more time than anything else. But what Sarah enjoyed was *performing*. They did three takes of the scene where she argued with Brett and each one was different. It was the excitement of never knowing exactly what was going to happen next which made the job so exciting.

One thing disturbed her. As Sarah walked off, she passed an actor who looked naggingly familiar. He was tall and thin, with his hair tied back, because he was dressed as a waiter. Sarah tried to figure out where she had seen him before, but wasn't sure.

Luke caught up with her as she was going into her trailer to get changed. He was still in his tuxedo. His curly brown hair was tousled. He looked just like he did in the first film she had seen him in: *Cool College*.

She stopped on the steps of the trailer.

"I didn't get the chance to thank you properly for what you did yesterday," she told him. She had slept most of the time since then. Luke shrugged.

"It was nothing. Anyone else would have done the same. I just happened to get there first."

"It didn't feel like nothing to me."

Luke gave her a sincere smile. "Maybe I offset the lousy impression I made the other night, at least."

"I already forgave you for that."

"Good." His smile became more raffish. "Then let me take a chance on our getting to know each other better. I've heard about a little restaurant about five miles from here. Good food, very quiet. We could go there tonight."

Sarah hesitated long enough to make it seem like she had to think about it. "I'm busy tonight," she lied.

"Tomorrow then. The day after's a rest day. We could stay out as late as we wanted."

Sarah continued to hesitate. "Do you promise to be on your best behaviour?" she asked.

"I promise."

"Then I guess I owe you a date."

Back in her room, Sarah got changed slowly, thinking about what she should wear the next evening – which dress, which perfume. Or maybe it would be more cool to put on casual clothes, make it look like she went out with big Hollywood movie stars every day of the week.

Every so often, Sarah had moments where her life stopped seeming real to her. This was one of them. A year ago, she was taking her GCSEs. A date with Luke Kelly was the kind of daydream that she and her friends confessed to in giggly, girly conversations. All sorts of men had asked Sarah out over the last year, but she'd turned them all down. There hadn't been one of them that she really liked, who had made her feel the way she felt this minute.

There was a knock on her door. Sarah put down the dress she was holding.

"Who is it?"

"Jon."

She let her brother in.

"They sent me with some new pages from the script."

Sarah finished brushing her hair. She remembered that she still hadn't found the script she misplaced earlier.

"What are they like?"

"I haven't read them. I'm not meant to."

Sarah turned round. "I wouldn't have minded. Leave them on the bed. I'll look at them later."

Jon stared at her, then glanced at the bed. "Nice dress. Going out somewhere?"

"Luke's taking me to a restaurant tomorrow."

Jon looked uncomfortable. "How could you date him, after what he did the other night?"

Sarah wished she hadn't told her brother. Jon was overprotective when it came to boyfriends. He didn't think anyone was good enough for his sister and this made her angry.

"It isn't really up to you who I go out with, is it? Remember how you kept trying to put me off your friend Gareth, and Steve Mackay too, when he asked me out?"

"That was years ago. They were . . ."

Sarah interrupted. "This is my life, Jon. Get your own. You seemed to get on well with that extra, Mary, today. Why don't you see what she's up to?"

"I just can't understand you going out with someone who cuts the heads off chickens."

"He didn't do it himself," Sarah retorted. "And what's the big deal about it? The chickens were going to die anyway. You were going to eat one of them. Or have you become a vegetarian overnight, like me? If I can let it go, why can't you?"

Jon threw his hands in the air and walked out, leaving the new script pages on the bed. Sarah felt upset for a while, but managed to talk herself out of it. He was a little jealous, that was all. It was understandable. Jon might deny it to himself, but he couldn't help being jealous of her success. Sarah's getting into films made it all worse. Films were the one thing Jon knew about and she didn't.

Now Sarah had discovered that she could act. If

she was in Jon's shoes, she'd probably feel a bit sick about it, too. But she'd make it right. Jon ought to see that her movie career was an opportunity for him, not a problem. And if he thought she was going to turn down a date with Luke Kelly, who had saved her life, because of one silly practical joke, he had another think coming.

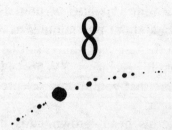

8

Heads turned as Luke and Sarah walked towards their secluded corner table.

"You're being recognized," Sarah told Luke.

"Nonsense," the film star replied. "You're the one they're interested in."

"I'm not that well known."

"Maybe. Maybe not. But the way you look tonight, every guy in the room wants to know you better, and every woman in the room wishes that she was you."

He sat down opposite her, wearing his T-shirt and jeans. Maybe that was what people were really looking at, Sarah thought: a scruffy young man in a restaurant which normally required a jacket and tie. She had opted for a white linen dress with box pleats, the kind of classic which was neither formal nor casual. To her delight, Luke couldn't keep his eyes off her.

"I want to know all about you," he said, after ordering the wine. "Your full life story."

Sarah gave him an edited version. Her first sixteen years took about two minutes to recount.

"Then, in the last year, things started to change."

Luke raised his eyebrows. "Whoa! Hold on! Are you telling me that you're only seventeen?"

"That's right."

He shook his head, brown curls floating over his eyebrows. "You're incredible, you know that? You're going to be huge. Only seventeen. I thought that *I* made it when *I* was young."

"How old were you when you made your first picture?"

"Eighteen. Nineteen when it came out, but I claimed to be twenty. You know how it is with guys. We always want to be older than we really are." He paused. "But we're still talking about you. How did it happen? One minute you're – what did you call it? *A catalogue girl*. The next you're all over fashion magazines, on the cover of *Vogue*, practically a supermodel . . ."

"Just like that."

"Just like that. How?" Luke asked, as he poured champagne.

Sarah shrugged. "I got lucky. I guess . . . I was in

the right place at the right time. I thought I'd grown too tall, too gawky. I didn't have a big enough chest. But then older girls with a similar kind of look started to make it, and everyone was looking round for younger, new faces with the same kind of appeal. There I was. It was very exciting, but kind of unnerving, too. You dream about something like that happening to you, but when it does, you're too busy to appreciate how glamorous it all is. It just feels like hard work."

"I know what you mean."

"Sometimes I get jealous of my friends. They're at college, they have normal lives, boyfriends . . . no pressure. Most of them haven't even thought about a job yet. While here I am, constantly making career moves, like this movie. We can't relate to each other any more. I go back and see them, but it's not the same. I know I've lost them."

Luke nodded sympathetically. "Some people take time out, go to college, pick up their career again later. Jodie Foster did it."

"Yes, and look what happened to her," Sarah replied. "She got stalked by some weirdo who ended up shooting a president. You can't go back, can you? You can't have fame and wealth and then pretend that it never happened."

Luke looked wistful. "I guess you're right," he said thoughtfully. "But I sure as hell keep trying."

"You must have had to grow up quickly too," she said, as their vichyssoise arrived.

"At first I loved it," he said. "I was hanging out with all these cool people. Women started throwing themselves at me. You know, I was a Chicago meat-packer's son, not one of the Hollywood brat pack. I thought I'd arrived in the land of plenty . . ." He sighed. "But the girls weren't so much interested in me as the guy on the silver screen. Then, after a while, the attention gets real wearing. You just want to hide. These days, the only women I date are actresses. The only friends I have are the people on whatever movie I'm working on at the time. Sometimes it gets a little lonely and I do crazy things, like the other night."

"Why don't you stop," Sarah suggested, "take a rest for a while?"

Luke leant forward and stroked her hand. "I wouldn't know what to do with myself."

Sarah withdrew her hand and ate some more of her chilled soup. "You're being silly. You'd find things to do."

"Maybe if I had someone like you with me."

Sarah smiled sympathetically. She was on the verge of being bowled over by Luke, yet part of her remained cynical. She might be falling for his standard lonely movie star chat-up line, so she gazed into his clear blue eyes and tried to sound sensible.

"Maybe you need to get away on your own first – find yourself – before you're ready to get into a real relationship."

Luke nodded. "Maybe you're right. When I've finished the film I've got lined up after this one, maybe I'll do just that."

They finished their soup in silence. As soon as the waiter had taken their plates away, a middle-aged woman came over to the table holding a menu.

"I hope you don't mind," she said to Luke, "but my teenage daughter is such a big fan of yours. She'll be so excited when we tell her we saw you. Would you sign this?"

Luke's eyes narrowed. "Don't you know *any-thing*?" he snapped. "You *never* interrupt stars for autographs until they've finished their meal. Aren't I entitled to a little privacy?"

The woman blushed a deep scarlet and turned away. Sarah felt embarrassed and angry with Luke.

"If you don't go after that woman this moment and apologize," she hissed at him, "I'm walking out of this restaurant right now!"

Luke looked shocked. Without speaking, he got up and went after the woman. Sarah could hear him grovelling, asking for the name of the woman's daughter. He came back.

"It wasn't for her daughter, you know. I could tell. It was for her."

"Who cares?" Sarah said, trying not to raise her voice. "And how can you possibly know? You're so arrogant it amazes me. Two years ago, if my mother had seen you in a restaurant, I'd have killed her if she hadn't tried to get your autograph for me."

"Really?" Luke said. "You were a fan?"

Sarah blushed. "Sort of. There's nothing wrong with being a fan."

"You're right," Luke said. "You know something?"

"What?"

"You're the most real person I've met in years."

He leant forward, nearly singeing his long hair over the flame from the candle. Then he moved the candlestick aside and kissed her, full on the lips. Sarah hesitated for a moment, then kissed him back. It was a long, heavy kiss, which lasted until the food came. Sarah sensed the presence of the waiter, discreetly keeping his distance with their next course in his hands. She pulled gently away and Luke smiled sweetly. No one had ever kissed Sarah that way before. Somehow, she knew that nothing would ever be the same again.

9

Jon walked up to the director's trailer. He was about to knock when he heard the argument going on inside.

"You've ruined the whole thing! What did you think you were doing?"

"It's my call. There's nothing you can do about it."

"You don't think so? Suppose I go to the studio, tell them what you're doing? You think they'll like it if you end up killing the girl?"

"Like I told you, I haven't made my mind up yet."

"What's to make up? Either you . . ."

A voice spoke in Jon's ear.

"Interesting conversation?" Luke Kelly asked.

Jon was embarrassed. "I . . . er . . . had a message for Mr Fitzgerald. Now doesn't seem to be a good time."

Kelly nodded. "Sounds like you're right. I had a meeting arranged with Leo, but, heck! Want to go get a beer?"

"Sure."

Jon joined the American in the hospitality trailer. A week had passed since the incident in the dining room, and there had been no more bad jokes. Luke had been out with Jon's sister twice. Jon wasn't happy about it, but so far the actor seemed to be treating Sarah well.

"Are you enjoying the shoot?" Luke asked Jon, passing him a chilled bottle of Rolling Rock.

"It's hard work," Jon said, "but it's interesting. Leo's fascinating to watch. A lot of the time, he seems to be making it up as he goes along. It's exciting."

"That's right," Luke told him. "There aren't many like him left – none at all in Hollywood. They'll drop him soon."

"Is the business that cruel?" Jon asked.

"Crueller. A handful of directors and stars get big enough to do exactly what they want. But if they relax and have a few flops, the past counts for nothing. Same goes for actors."

"So what keeps you going?"

Luke shrugged. "I'm small fry, expendable.

There's another like me along every summer – great pecs, fresh-faced. We have a life expectancy of about five years. Then you can try and go for bigger, more legit roles, like Tom Cruise, or you can take the James Dean route."

"'Live fast, die young, leave a pretty corpse'?"

"That's the one. I'm really hacked off with doing *Cool College* sequels. The film wasn't much good in the first place, but the last two really sucked."

"Why do you have to be in them, then? Couldn't you refuse?"

Luke shook his head. "I signed this stupid restrictive contract when I was eighteen. My agent keeps trying to renegotiate it, but . . ." He shrugged his shoulders. Jon saw the locations manager walking towards the trailer. It was time to get back to work.

As Jon walked past the director's trailer, a bearded man with dark hair and sunglasses walked out. He had to be from Hollywood, Jon figured. Who else wore shades on an overcast day? Jon decided to use this moment to deliver the message from the locations manager. However, before he could get over to the trailer, Sarah ran over, sheets of pink paper scrunched up in her hand. She didn't see Jon, but walked straight into Fitzgerald's trailer, without knocking.

Jon didn't want to eavesdrop, but he couldn't help hearing the first part of the conversation.

"How can you do this to me? We had a distinct verbal agreement. My agent assured me . . ."

"Come on, Sarah. You've revealed more than I'm asking on modelling jobs. Professionals think of their bodies as tools, not possessions . . ."

"Hold it right there!" Sarah interrupted the director. Jon was impressed by his sister's attitude, the way she was standing up to Fitzgerald. "Don't start throwing that *you're a professional and it's only a body* routine at me," Sarah shouted. "It's my body! I own it. I'm not doing this for you, or for anybody, ever! Got it?"

Jon didn't hear Fitzgerald's reply, but he did hear the obscenity his sister threw back at him before she walked out of Leo's trailer and stalked over to her own, oblivious to Jon's presence.

Jon knocked on Fitzgerald's door.

"What is it?"

"Urgent message."

"Come."

"Oh," said Fitzgerald, as Jon entered the room. "It's you." He took the note, read it, and threw it in the bin. Jon turned to go.

"Tell me," said Fitzgerald. "I have half a dozen up and coming American actresses begging me to play the girl torn between Brett Johnson and Luke Kelly, but I go for your sister, give her a big break. Even give her brother a job too."

"So?"

"So, how come she won't lose her clothes for a couple of scenes? Why can't I get her to understand that this isn't art, it's business? I have to sell this movie. And her body is what every hot-blooded American male over the age of thirteen will want to see."

"Was nudity in the script?" Jon asked, politely.

Fitzgerald looked angry. "We're not shooting the script. We're shooting the movie that I want to make."

"But if it's not the movie that Sarah thought she was making, then she's got a point, hasn't she?"

Fitzgerald became angry. "Your sister is a no-talent, minor model who got lucky because we happened to need someone who looked like her. And if she doesn't do whatever is necessary to get this picture made, then she's going to be on the scrap heap before she's old enough to vote!"

Jon didn't know what to say. He admired Fitzgerald, and had nothing against sex on the screen. It seemed hypocritical to him that films could show violence in gory detail but weren't allowed to portray the human body doing something much more natural. But Sarah was his sister. He didn't want to watch her cavorting with Luke Kelly on screen any more than he had to.

"Is there any reply to that message?" he asked, sullenly.

Fitzgerald growled. "Tell him we can discuss the fire scene after dinner tonight."

"OK. 'Bye."

Jon went over to Sarah's trailer. The door was half open. He'd go in and talk it over with her. Then he saw that Sarah wasn't alone. Luke Kelly was with her.

"He told me I was a lousy actress," Sarah was moaning. "He told me he only hired me for my body."

"You know that's not true," Kelly comforted her. "Everyone says how natural you are, how convincing. He was trying to wind you up so that you'd do what he wants, that's all."

"Why should I have to strip off? It's not in my contract."

"Relax," Luke said. "I'll see him for you, sort it out. If the scene's necessary, he can always get a body double for you."

"Would you talk to him? I'd really appreciate that."

"Of course."

Kelly leant over and put his arms round Jon's sister. They began kissing. Jon backed off as quietly and as quickly as he could manage, bumping into someone as he did.

It was Mary, the actress who'd been his partner in the ballroom scene.

"What are you?" she asked him. "A detective or

a pervert?"

Jon smiled awkwardly. He recognized the film dialogue which Mary was teasing him with.

"That's for me to know and you to find out," he replied.

"She's your sister, isn't she?" Mary said. "I'm sorry I bad-mouthed her the other day. I was wrong about her and Leo, anyhow."

"You were."

Mary grinned coquettishly. "She was saving herself for a bigger catch." She walked off, leaving Jon in embarrassed silence. He often found himself in situations like this – on the edge of things, observing. *Never eavesdrop*, his mother had once warned him. *You'll overhear things you're better off not knowing*. Maybe that applied to all three of the conversations he'd overheard this afternoon. Did Fitzgerald really think that Sarah couldn't act? Jon thought she was good, but he was hardly an objective witness, and neither was Luke. Did Luke really care about his sister? Or was he just using her? Would he drop her as soon as the shoot was over?

Jon was so wrapped up in his thoughts that he didn't notice Slacker until the scruffy youth was alongside him outside the canteen.

"How's it going?" Slacker asked. "Know if there are any more crowd scenes I could get a part in?"

"Just one," Jon told him. "They're filming the

wedding tomorrow. If you go along to the casting director, they might be short of a body or two."

"Thanks. I appreciate your help. You're Sarah Wood's brother, aren't you?"

"How did you find that out?"

"I hear things. Is it true she's dating Luke Kelly?"

Jon replied curtly with a question of his own. "Are you working for the press?"

Slacker looked affronted. "No. I swear."

"Whatever," Jon said. "It's none of your business."

Jon walked away, thinking about the conversation he'd overheard between Leo and the bearded man – the one about the girl dying. What had it meant? Still, there was no point in getting obsessive about it. This was only a movie, after all. Then he thought about Karen and the exploding boat. He had to watch everything that was going on very carefully, very carefully indeed.

He walked up to the Hall to help prepare for his sister's wedding.

August

10

As the shoot went on, some of the tensions of the first few days seemed to dissolve. Sarah's agent, Sally, negotiated a compromise over the nude scenes the director wanted. A body double would be used for one of Sarah's love scenes with Luke, while she would remain partially clothed for the other. Jon was relieved.

Sarah was still going out with Luke. Jon had to get used to the fact that he wasn't going to see much of his sister any more. The closeness he thought they had was illusory, he now realized. It made him angry at first, but he'd learn to cope with it. Jon used to con himself that he was happy about Sarah's success. Now he knew that he'd been lying to himself because he didn't want to admit how alienated they were from each other. They didn't inhabit the same planet any more, and it was pointless to pretend otherwise.

Anyway, Sarah spent all her free time with Luke Kelly. As Melissa and Aidan's relationship developed onscreen, so the couple became inseparable off-screen. Sarah insisted that Luke was different when you got to know him, that being with her was changing him. Jon affected disinterest. After a few weeks, he avoided conversations with his sister. He spent a lot of time hanging out with Todd, picking up tricks of the trade, gossip, stories – anything that might be useful to him in the future.

Occasionally, Jon managed to slide into conversation with Leo Fitzgerald. You could learn a lot just by hanging around Leo. The director encouraged Jon a little. Now and then he would tease the boy over his curiosity about the unfinished script.

"You know who I learnt a lot from? Roger Corman – the master of the quickie. He could make a film in two days, using recycled sets from the film before. For him, a two-week shoot was a luxury and everyone doubled up their jobs. You know what he used to say about a script? *'What you need is a very good first reel, because people want to know what's going on. Then you need a very good last reel, because people want to know how it all turns out. Everything else doesn't matter.'*"

"You don't believe that?" Jon asked.

"It's probably the best sense I've ever heard in the movies."

Jon wasn't sure if the director was winding him up or not.

When he wasn't around Todd or the director, Jon spent some time with Mary. The actress had been half-promised a small speaking part which was being newly written into the screenplay.

"They're not paying me at the moment," she told Jon, "but I've got free bed and board. It's more fun than sharing a flat with four other actresses in Neasden."

Jon and Mary went out for pub lunches on rest days. At times, they seemed like a couple. Yet, somehow, they never progressed beyond parting pecks on the lips. Jon had never had a serious girl-friend. Mary seemed willing at times, but nothing ever came of it. Maybe it was her, not wanting to throw her pretty self away on a penurious student. Or maybe it was him, avoiding a relationship for reasons which he couldn't put words to, but had something to do with his sister and Luke Kelly.

Soon the final week of shooting approached. Leo was precisely on schedule. So far, all of the film had been shot on location, but the scene they were shooting today could only be done in the studio. Leo had hired Shepherd's Gate, an old studio on the edge of London, an hour's drive from Bradlington. Jon gathered that the director had got a cheap deal because the studio was about to be shut down and demolished.

The studio sound stage was shabby and decrepit. As the crew cleaned up over the weekend, they sneezed endlessly in the dust which had settled everywhere. By Sunday night, Jon felt like he'd crawled through a desert, but the set was in place and ready to be set on fire.

Leo had lived up to his half-promise. Mary had landed a speaking part as Jane, an old friend of Melissa's. Now the two of them were sitting in a replica of Melissa's room at Bradlington Hall. This scene was taking place just before the wedding, as Jane helped Melissa into her wedding dress.

"You look gorgeous," Jane said. "I'm so happy for you."

"Thanks for agreeing to be a bridesmaid at such short notice," Melissa told her. "You saved my life."

"Believe me," Jane said, "I wouldn't have missed this for anything."

Then she paused, noticing the tear which was dripping down onto Melissa's white dress.

"Melissa, what is it? What's wrong?"

Melissa turned her tear-stained eyes to Jane.

"I can't get it out of my mind. Suppose Aidan's been telling the truth? Suppose Matthew did murder all his other wives? Suppose I'm next?"

Jane gave her a hug, then handed her a tissue.

"You know you're being silly," she said. "Matthew's been unlucky, but all three of his wives died in accidents. They weren't murdered. And Aidan's been psychologically disturbed since he was a child. Matthew showed you the doctor's reports. That's why he didn't invite him to the wedding, in case he does something crazy."

"But maybe Aidan's right," Melissa protested. "Maybe I'm the one acting crazy, marrying someone thirty years older than me."

"Either you love him or you don't," Jane told her. "Age doesn't come into it."

Jon watched the monitor as the camera closed in on Sarah's face, showing the doubt in her eyes. How could anyone say that she couldn't act?

"Cut!" Leo Fitzgerald called. "OK, that's a wrap. Let's get on with setting up the fire scene."

Jon hurried into action. This was the most complicated set-up in the film. Minutes after Melissa and Matthew exchanged vows, his sister would be trapped in her room when the building caught fire. All of the other guests would get out. Then Aidan, after an argument with Matthew, would charge back into the building and save Melissa's life.

"Now do you believe me?" he would ask, once they were outside. But Melissa would still be uncertain, knowing that someone set the fire up, but not knowing whether it was the father or the son.

The actual wedding scene had been shot weeks

earlier at the stately home. To keep location costs to a minimum, Fitzgerald arranged for the couple to marry in the mansion's chapel, then have the reception in the house. The set had been decorated to look like the house they were supposed to be in. Carpenters had built a mock-up of the west wing. Beyond Sarah's room were two corridors and a staircase. The shots of guests watching the fire from outside would be faked later, using visual overlays during the editing.

The trick with fire scenes, Leo Fitzgerald explained to the crew, was not to burn the actual sets, but to burn the plastic gunk which they had spread over the walls. Timing was crucial. If the first take went wrong, you were left with scorched walls. Two special effects people would have to put out the fires, repaint the walls, then wait for the paint to dry before spreading the flammable gunk all over them again. But the crew only had a day to shoot the whole thing, and it was already getting on for noon.

Sarah sat in the part of the set which was her dressing room, looking calm. Mary, the extra who had landed the part of the bridesmaid, was on the edge of the set. She had a short scene with Luke Kelly, who was going to go into the fire himself. Fitzgerald had offered Kelly a stuntman double, but Luke wouldn't hear of it.

Jon got onto the crane which was holding the

camera for the overhead shots. The previous day he'd been given a temporary promotion, to Camera Assistant, when the woman whose job it was had come down with appendicitis. Jon wouldn't get a credit for this, as he wasn't in the union, but he'd be able to tell people precisely which scenes he'd helped to shoot.

The job wasn't very difficult but Jon took it seriously. He was responsible for the safety of the camera and maintaining the level of film stock. He was tired, having stayed up late the night before, reading the manual, then arriving early this morning to make sure he was fully confident with the equipment.

As the crane lifted into the air, Jon saw Slacker, wearing technician's overalls, standing by a row of fire extinguishers. The youth must have talked his way into a job on the safety crew. Sarah had insisted on maximum safety for this scene and Leo had assured her that there was no risk. Near Slacker, Brett was getting into his position on one of the corridor sets. Who started the fire? Brett or Luke? No one knew. Fitzgerald still hadn't revealed how he intended to end the film. Jon wondered whether the director had even made up his own mind yet.

"We're going for everything in one take," Fitzgerald announced over the tannoy. "This scene's the fulcrum of the film. I want to do this in real time, and I expect you all to be covered in real sweat by the time it's over. I don't want anyone to panic, no matter how hairy things look down there. We've got all the safety angles covered. Now, help me get the shots I need to make this movie a masterpiece. I know we can do it.

"Ready?" the director went on, a little nervousness in his voice. "OK. Everybody into position. Action!"

11

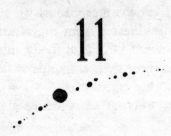

Sarah waited patiently for the scene to begin. This was her most complicated scene, even though she didn't have to learn any lines for it. Mainly she had to react – to the smoke coming in through the door, to the flames surrounding her in the corridor. She had to look out of a window and consider whether to jump. Luke, meanwhile, would fight his way through the flames and carry her to safety, just as she seemed about to be overcome by the smoke.

Luke's part in the film was nearly over. He had to leave a week before the end of the shoot in order to start work on his next film, *Cool College 5*, which he wasn't looking forward to.

"Why don't you join me," he'd said to her last

night, "as soon as this shoot is over? You could fly to L.A., stay at my house in the valley. We'd have a great time."

"You'd be working," she protested.

"No one works that hard in L.A. Making movies there isn't like it is here, with a slave-driver director. It's laid back."

"I'll think about it," Sarah told him, cautiously. "I do have some other assignments lined up. I'd have to talk to my agent."

"You don't want to carry on as a model after this," Luke insisted. "Come to L.A. with me. Stay as long as you like. I'll introduce you to people. You'll get lots of offers, I promise."

Sarah was so lost in her thoughts that she didn't hear Leo call "Action!" She noticed, though, when the walls were set alight, and she began to perform. Helped by a fan, smoke began to seep beneath the door in the room where Sarah sat. The crew filmed Sarah's reaction shots quickly. Then, when the flames had built up enough, the camera moved in to a medium close-up of her opening the door, seeing the flames, and being driven back by the heat.

The heat from the flames was real. It shocked Sarah. Never mind Luke being offered a stunt double, maybe she should have one for herself. She went to the window, opened it, and screamed for help. The actual sound of the scream didn't matter, as it would be re-dubbed later. She backed into the room. Now she just had to wait for Luke, coming to rescue her.

Off stage, Sarah heard Luke being given his instruction to get into position. He had a conflict with Matthew first of all, which ended with Aidan knocking his father out in the middle of the flames. Sarah could barely make out their dialogue above the sound of the fire. It was hard to believe that the plastic stuff they'd been spreading on the walls could make so much noise.

The fire was very realistic. Flames were even beginning to lick their way across the front of the sound stage. No one had told Sarah that this was going to happen. Unless . . . Sarah backed up against the wall . . . suppose it was going wrong? But no, she was an actress. There was a camera crew a few metres away from her and Leo had gone over the stringent safety checks with her only minutes ago. She mustn't panic, mustn't spoil the take, or it would be hours before they could start again.

From above, it seemed to Jon that the fire was getting out of control. Fitzgerald kept on filming regardless. Sarah wasn't in any danger, but the fire in the corridors was way too strong – the actual sets were on fire and smoke was building up. Still, the camera kept rolling. Sarah continued to act, despite the fact that, at the edge of the set, Luke had walked off and was arguing with the director.

"I can't go through that! It's too hot!"

"Don't be a wimp," Fitzgerald told him. "Now, go!"

Luke moved back into camera shot. Brett was still lying on the floor where Luke had knocked him out earlier. In a moment he would be able to get up, as the camera followed Luke across the set.

But when the camera followed Luke, Brett didn't get up. The smoke must have got to him. And the fire was dangerously near, too. Flames were building up around the whole stage now. It was becoming an inferno. In her room at the side of the set, sweat poured down Sarah's wedding dress. Meanwhile, Luke was trying to make his way across the set. He climbed a burning staircase. Then he crossed the first corridor, starting as he burnt his arm by brushing it against a wall.

It was impossible to see what was going on in the final corridor. Smoke billowed through, flooding the room where Sarah waited.

"This is ridiculous," Jon shouted into the intercom. "Luke and Sarah are in danger! Get them out!"

But the little red light on the intercom didn't come on and Jon realized that the electrics were probably out, too. If this went on much longer, the entire studio would be ablaze.

The smoke was building up. Sarah knew that there were always delays, that time was certain to stretch out when you were stuck in a room with smoke pouring in at you, beginning to fear for your life. Yet she *must* be safe. There were people all around her – the crew. There were trained fire fighters. Or were there? She couldn't remember. She couldn't think. On a signal from Ruth, the assistant director, Sarah was meant to collapse. But she couldn't see Ruth any more and pretty soon she wouldn't have to fake collapsing. The room she was in didn't have a flammable coating, but it had started to burn. All the smoke and heat were getting to her. It was hard to stay upright.

Jon nudged Jo, the camera operator, in the back. She looked around saying, "What is it?"

"We've got to get down! My sister and Luke are in danger!"

Jo shook her head. "It just looks that way. It's meant to. If there's a problem, the people on the ground will sort it out. Leo'll kill me if I don't get all of this."

"But there's nothing to see! There's too much smoke."

"They're great atmospherics, that's all."

"Look, Jo, that's my sister down there . . ."

He reached for the lever which would lower the crane. Jo turned round, giving Jon the coldest stare he had ever received in his life.

"This is the movies, Jon. If you wreck a shot without permission from the director, you'll never work in the business again!"

Jon shook his head.

"Just keep filming," he said, as he pulled the lever. "I'll take the responsibility if Leo complains."

Smoke billowed out from beneath them. It was already unbearably hot. As the camera platform began to go down, Jon felt like he was descending into hell.

Luke didn't appear. Never had Sarah wanted to see someone so much in her life. Suppose he was in danger too? But she didn't have time to worry about him now. She had to worry about getting out of here.

"Help!" she called.

There was no response. Where was Luke? Where was her brother? She looked up for the camera on the crane. It was coming down towards her. If it came down close enough, she could climb onto the camera platform. They could whisk her out of here. But then the crane stopped, several metres above her head. What should she do? Perhaps the only thing for it was to run straight into the flames in front of her on the stage. Run for dear life to the safety of the crew. She could hear shouting off-stage. Somewhere, an alarm was sounding. Finally, they must have realized the risk.

There was movement now and for a moment Sarah thought that she was saved. She began to walk towards the sound. That was when she realized that she couldn't run anywhere, because her lungs were full of smoke. The moment she tried to walk in the direction of the sound, she fell to the floor, gagging for breath.

But it was better on the floor. There was less smoke. She could breathe a little. And there was someone coming towards her – only a shadow in the smoke, but it was getting nearer. She tried to make a noise, to call out. She hoped that whoever it was could see her. The shadow was getting closer, closer.

And then, with a gasp of horror, Sarah saw the shadow's face: it had long, singed, fair hair and wore a horrible yellow plastic mask. Reaching out for her, the shadowy figure seemed to wear a sickly, terrifying grin. Sarah tried to defend herself, but it was no good – she had no energy left to strike out or run away. He was going to get her.

She passed out.

Jo swung the camera platform back away from the set. They had got in close to Sarah, but then began to choke on the smoke. Flames licked the camera as the alarm sounded below. Finally, people were springing into action.

"We're getting out!" Jo told him. "Otherwise the heat will damage the film!"

"At least let me down," Jon insisted.

"OK, OK. We must have enough footage now."

Jon could see movement on the set as he jumped off the platform and ran towards it. People were using fire extinguishers, but the flames were too strong. A few metres from the fire, Ruth, the assistant director, was reviving Brett Johnson. Of Luke and Sarah there was no sign.

Jon ran towards the part of the set where his sister should be. It was a blazing inferno. Parts of the set were collapsing. Another part was burnt out. How could a competent director allow this to happen? Fitzgerald was nowhere to be seen. Then a figure began to crawl out of the flames, dragging something behind him. It was a tall, ghostly figure, with long, scorched hair and a yellow mask. Suddenly, Jon realized that it was Slacker, and the person he was dragging was Sarah. Jon ran forward to help him.

Slacker pulled the mask off as the nurse ran towards them. "She only just passed out," he said. "She was conscious when I got to her."

The nurse began to give Sarah oxygen. Slacker looked wrecked, even paler than usual, and scared. Jon put his arms around him.

"You did brilliantly. You saved her life."

The youth nodded distractedly. "I'd better get cleaned up," he said.

Jon returned to Sarah. Her eyes opened. "What happened?" she moaned.

"The fire got out of control," the nurse explained. "But you're all right now."

Sarah sat up and looked around. "Where's Luke?"

As she spoke, her boyfriend walked out of the burnt-out part of the set, supported by Leo Fitzgerald. His clothes and hair were scorched and his face was covered with black carbon, but he didn't look as bad as Sarah. She stood up.

"Thank God you're all right!" she said, hugging him close to her.

"You look like Miss Havisham," he told her.

"Save that for the camera," Leo told them. "I want to get you two straight back to the house, looking just the way you are now. We'll film Luke carrying you out of the west wing. It'll be really authentic."

"I think these two need checking at a hospital," the nurse warned. "The smoke may have damaged their lungs."

Fitzgerald looked at Luke and Sarah. "They can stand, can't they?" he asked. "Come on, the show must go on!"

While the nurse treated Sarah and Luke, Jon accosted the director. "You can't just walk away from this! Sarah nearly died. If it hadn't been for this guy here . . ." He looked for Slacker to point him out, but the long-haired youth had gone.

"Listen," said Fitzgerald. "The fire got out of control. I'm sorry. It's a risk we take. But don't exaggerate the danger. We got some great footage . . ."

He turned to Jo. "Everything all right your end, Jo? Your monitor lead burnt out."

"Fine," she said. "No thanks to my new assistant."

Leo turned back to Jon. In the distance, he could hear fire engines. Jon wanted to complain about Sarah being forced to drive to the hall and do the next scene, but he had stuck his neck out far enough already. Fitzgerald turned round.

"Here's the fire brigade. I thought we'd disconnected all the alarms, but we set off the ones in the next studio. Ruth can liaise with them. I have a film to finish."

The fire was starting to die down, mainly because everything that would burn was already burnt. It was odd, Jon thought, the way that the front of the sound stage had caught fire, almost as though someone had planned to trap the people inside.

As Jon looked closely at the fire, he thought he saw something, right at the back of the set, where it had been strongest: a large can, of the type used to hold petrol. But maybe it was meant to be there.

"Was all of this accidental?" he asked Ruth, who

was watching the fire brigade trail a hose in. "It got strong awfully quickly."

The assistant director shrugged.

"I haven't seen one go up as quickly as that before," she said. "But all the wood in this place is ancient, and dry as a tinder box. It's a good thing they're demolishing it, or the rebuilding costs would be huge."

"Did you use petrol to light it?"

"You're kidding!" Ruth said. "That would make it burn too strong and way too fast."

"Isn't that exactly what happened?"

Ruth shook her head. "Leo may be headstrong and obsessive, but he isn't stupid enough to risk burning people to death deliberately."

The remains of the blaze were quickly put out. Jon watched with Sarah until Luke came and told her that it was time for them to drive to Bradlington Hall. When she'd gone, Jon followed the fire-fighters into the charred scenery, intending to point out the petrol can he'd seen earlier.

It was no longer there.

Had Jon imagined it, or had someone removed the can while he was talking to Ruth? What motive would anyone have for making the fire worse than it was? Jon didn't know. All he did know was that there had been too many accidents on this film shoot and this was one too many. Any two of the three could have been coincidence, but, taken together, they formed a pattern. Who was at the centre of it?

12

They had finished filming the rescue scene at Bradlington Hall and Sarah was exhausted. She couldn't believe that Leo had insisted on filming the brief shot of Luke carrying her out of the hall on the same day as she had nearly burnt to death. But he had done so, even though it meant filming in late afternoon, when the light was poor.

Now Sarah lay in Luke's arms on her bed. Luke had been less affected by the fire earlier. He kissed her passionately, but Sarah felt too wasted to respond. Seeing how frazzled she was, he began to massage her back.

"That's nice," Sarah murmured, "very nice."

"Why won't you come back to the States with me?" Luke asked after a while. This wasn't the first time he'd asked her the question but Sarah still wasn't sure how to reply.

"I've only known you for a month. How can I throw everything in and just come after you?"

"Why not?"

"I want you to respect me, Luke. I have a career. I'm independent. I'd like to come and visit you, but on my terms."

"Fine. I do respect you. What are your terms?"

"That you stop putting all this pressure on me and let me come in my own time. Also, I'd like you to meet my parents."

Luke turned over. "*Meet your parents?* Are you kidding? You make me feel like I'm fifteen years old."

Sarah explained. "I'm only seventeen. I still live at home, in a sense. I'm not there much, but my mum and dad like to know who I'm with. They feel more comfortable if they've met them. What's so odd about that?"

Luke shrugged. "Nothing, I guess. OK, anything you say. I'll meet your parents. But don't make me wait long. Come soon. Come quickly. I want to show you my beach house. I want to take you for moonlit walks on the beach at Malibu."

"I'd like that," Sarah whispered, kissing him softly on the lips. "You know I would."

"I've got some good news," Luke went on. "Leo has lent me his car for the rest day tomorrow. He's staying in the hotel and working on the end of the script."

"You mean he still hasn't worked it out?"

"No. The screenwriter came over with the re-writes but Leo threw half of them out. Thing is, he's only got me for three more days, so he has to get the ending worked out quickly or he'll end up paying a lot extra for pick-up shots back at Burbank."

"Pick-up shots?"

"They're bits that are filmed later to fill in gaps in the story, or because things didn't come out. The point is that he doesn't need his car tomorrow. Come for a drive with me."

"I'd love to."

"Good."

She kissed him again.

"I love you," he murmured into her ear.

"I love you too," she whispered back.

There was no point in holding out any longer. They had come through a fire together. Sarah had a feeling that they might just go through the rest of their lives together, too.

"Seen this?"

Todd handed Jon one of the tabloid Sunday newspapers as he was eating his breakfast. The front page headline was:

"SUPERMODEL AND SUPERBRAT!"

The sub-heading read, "Romance *flares up* for

model superstar Sarah Wood and teen heart-throb Luke Kelly after he saves her life *twice!*" The story beneath was salacious and inaccurate. It credited Luke, not Slacker, with pulling Sarah out of the fire, and made Luke's saving Sarah from drowning sound a lot more brave and dramatic than it had been. Maybe Luke *had* saved her life, Jon thought, but she was near land and there were a lot of other people just behind him.

"Suspicious, isn't it?" Todd said.

"How do you mean?"

"All those insider quotes, like 'Friends say they've never seen Luke so happy.' What friends? 'Close family confide that Luke is Sarah's first real love.' Have you been talking to the *News of the Screws*?"

Jon shook his head.

"Of course you haven't. It all comes out of the mouth of Kelly's publicist. He's given her the whole story, or Fitzgerald has." Todd scratched his head. "Makes you wonder though."

"What?"

"That fire yesterday. You were there. Did it look like an accident to you? Or do you think it was set up to make Kelly look like a hero?"

Jon was lost for words. He hadn't seen Sarah since Slacker pulled her out of the fire. She never left Luke's side these days and Jon chose not to hang around them. Sarah probably didn't know who had saved her. Could Luke have taken the credit?

"Makes you think, doesn't it?" Todd said.

"Yes," Jon said. "It certainly does."

He decided to visit his sister, taking the newspaper with him.

When Jon got to her door, he found it open. He knocked anyway.

"Come in," said Luke Kelly's voice.

Kelly was standing by the window, in a brown, crumpled leather jacket, while Jon's sister brushed her hair.

"Jon, how you doing?" Kelly said.

"I wanted a word with Sarah."

"She's sitting right there."

Sarah turned round and gave Jon one of her dazzling smiles, the fake one she reserved for distant relatives and remote family friends. "What is it, Jon?"

"Can I have a word with you on your own for a minute?"

"I haven't got any secrets from Luke. And we're just about to go out for the day. Can it wait?"

Jon shrugged. "I guess. But you might want to give Mum and Dad a ring before they read this." He handed Sarah the paper, then turned to go out. Sarah said nothing, but Luke followed him into the corridor. Jon ignored him. Luke grabbed Jon roughly by the arm.

"What is it with you?" he said in a low growl. "I thought we were friends. But you seem to be trying to get between me and your sister."

"Then it doesn't look like I've been very successful, does it?" Jon replied. "And if you like my sister so much, how come you planted that story in the papers?"

"*Me?*" Luke retorted, incredulously. "I need publicity like I need a hole in the head. If you want to know the source of the story, talk to our precious director. All he cares about is media coverage: hype, hype, hype, and it doesn't matter how he gets it. But don't try to screw things up between me and Sarah. I can be a nasty enemy."

"That, I can believe," Jon said, breaking loose of the actor and returning downstairs to the crew, where he belonged.

13

Leo Fitzgerald drove a red two-seater MGB. It was a meticulously restored, open-top, vintage sports car. Sarah and Luke walked out into the car park in the hot August sun. The director was chatting with Brett Johnson. Leo dangled the keys in front of Luke.

"You take care of her, all right? Not one scratch, no dents, or I'll write you out of this movie."

"You're lending him that beauty?" Brett said, in disbelief. "I hope it's fully insured."

"It is, and so is Luke."

"Shouldn't you be indoors," Luke suggested, caustically, "fixing the script?"

"It's all happening in here," Leo said, pointing to his head. "Anyway, Brett's been giving me some ideas. Do you have any suggestions to make, Luke? Or you, Sarah?"

"You're paid to work out the ending," Luke told him. "Sarah and I are paid to make people believe it. C'mon, Sarah."

He took her arm. Sarah had an opinion or two of her own, but didn't feel like she could say anything now without appearing to disagree with Luke, so she didn't.

"We got a nice publicity puff out of you two in one of today's papers," Fitzgerald said. "Did you see it?"

"Not yet," Luke said.

"I . . ." Sarah began, but before she could get the sentence out, Brett interrupted her.

"Who is that guy over there? I keep seeing him around. Is he an extra, or what?"

Sarah looked where Brett was pointing. It was a long-haired youth she thought she'd seen before.

"I've noticed him," Sarah said. "Wasn't he one of the fire guards yesterday?"

"I've not hired him for anything," Fitzgerald said.

"Wasn't he an extra in the party scene?" Luke asked.

"I don't think so."

"Usually," Brett said, "people come and hang out by a movie set for an hour, two at the most. Then they see how slow everything is, get bored and go away."

"Except fans," Luke told them. "Or should I say *fanatics*. I sometimes get that in the States: creeps who hang around the location every minute of the day. You know the type – they haven't got a life of their own."

"That's rather sad," Sarah said.

"You mean pathetic," Luke told her. "It's not like autograph hunters – one signature and they're out of your face. People like that can make your life a misery. There was this girl once . . . aw, never mind. Let's frag him."

"What?"

"Get in the car."

Reluctantly, Sarah did as she was told. Luke started off the MG with a roar, then drove across the car park. The long-haired youth was walking away. He'd reached a deserted section at the far end of the car park. Luke sounded his horn and the youth glanced round.

"Now we'll have some fun," Luke told Sarah. He began to circle the youth with the MG, going faster and faster. The boy, who couldn't be much older than Sarah herself, looked frightened out of his wits. He tried to get out of the way of the car, but Luke kept widening and narrowing the circles.

"Stop it!" Sarah screamed. Luke ignored her.

"You're scaring him and you're scaring me!"

The youth's long, dirty-looking hair flew around

his face, covering his eyes. If he was unlucky, he would run straight into the car.

"Stop it!" Sarah insisted. "This is horrible!"

Luke ignored her again. The boy froze, seeing that there was no point in trying to get away. Luke began to slow down. Leo Fitzgerald was running over.

"Hey!" Luke called out, cruising up to the youth, "what's your problem?"

The youth was very thin and pale. Sarah wondered where he'd slept the night before.

"What do you want?" he asked, sounding defensive and scared.

"I want to know why you're hanging around my place of work," Luke told him.

"I want to know the same thing," Leo broke in. "Who are you?"

"I . . . I wanted to get a job on the film," the youth stuttered. "There weren't any going, but I kept turning up anyway."

"Where are you from?" Sarah asked, kindly.

"Ipswich."

"That's a long way to come."

"I think you'd better go back there," Fitzgerald told him, sternly. "This is a job of work we're doing, not a spectator sport. Come see the picture when it's released. Until then, go home. Otherwise I'll get security to throw you off the set any time you come near."

"I, I, uh . . ."

"Have you got any money?" Sarah asked.

The youth shook his head. She reached into her purse.

"Here," she said. "How much is the train fare?"

She'd been scared of the youth, but now she could see that he was just another loser. He'd done what people were supposed to do – travelled hundreds of kilometres in search of an opportunity, and found nothing.

"I . . . I don't know," said the young man. "I hitched."

"Put your money away," Fitzgerald told Sarah. He turned to the youth. "OK, you had a go at getting work. I respect that. But there's nothing here for you. We've done all the crowd scenes. We'll be wrapping the picture up in a few days. Now I want you gone. Actors get superstitious about strangers on set. So wait here. I'll get security to drive you to the station, buy you a ticket, put you on a train. All right?"

"All right," said the youth. "Thank you."

Then he turned to Sarah. "Thank you, too."

"You're welcome."

Sarah heard Leo giving instructions to the head of security, who apologized, explaining that they thought Slacker was on the crew. Then Luke revved the engine and they drove off at speed.

"Why were you so horrible to him?" Sarah asked.

"Wait until you've been in as many movies as I have," Luke lectured her. "You'll come to loathe cretins like that, too."

He put his foot down on the throttle. It bothered Sarah, the way Luke could call people "cretins". At times, he seemed to act as though he and people like him were on a different planet, where different rules applied. It wasn't right and she would tell him so. Over the last month, he seemed to have changed, to have become less callous. But suppose it was all an act put on for her behalf? Sarah tightened her safety belt.

"Where are we going?" she asked.

Luke turned to her and smiled. It was hard to be mad at him for long when it was a perfect summer's day and his brown, curly hair was blowing in the wind.

"Wait and see," he said, and pressed even further down on the accelerator.

Soon they had left the main road and were flying through country lanes. Despite the narrow, winding roads, Luke kept the speedometer hovering between fifty and sixty.

"Slow down," Sarah told him. "You're scaring me."

"This isn't fast," Luke insisted. "Wait till you see where I'm taking you."

Suddenly, he pressed hard on the brakes and

they swung off the country lane into a dirt road. A hand-painted sign by the turning read "Private".

"Where. . . ?"

"Mark, the locations manager, found this place. They couldn't use it, for one reason or another, but he told me about it."

The sports car bounced up and down, juddering uncomfortably on the rough track, which led up a steep hill. When they'd gone half a mile, they turned a corner and passed a sign which read *Danger! Proceed at your own risk*.

"Luke, I don't like this."

"If it's like Mark told me, you'll be amazed. Here we are."

Sarah stared at the spectacle below. They had arrived at the edge of a vast quarry. Winding paths were cut into sheer mountains of rock, latticed with caves. In places, the rock had crumbled away. In the middle of the quarry was a hollow filled with rubble, the result of occasional landslides.

"Leo was thinking of setting some kind of car chase here," Luke explained, "but the logistics were too difficult. You can't get into that hollow there. Let me show you what it would have been like."

He accelerated towards one of the cliffs.

"What did they used to mine here?" Sarah asked, trying to stay calm.

"Tin, maybe. Or copper. Or chalk. I dunno."

Dust blew around them as Luke drove onto a

track carved into the side of the cliff. The car was small, but even so, the road was less than a metre wider.

"Do you know where this comes out?" Sarah asked.

"Don't worry. It'll come out somewhere. Mark said he drove down it."

"In a car like this?"

"No. A landrover."

Luke speeded up the MG. It shuddered and shook as it hurtled along the rocky, narrow road.

"Luke, this is dangerous!" Sarah told him as they approached a blind corner.

"Hey, I do my own stunt driving. Didn't you know that?"

"Let's go back," Sarah pleaded, holding onto his arm for safety.

Luke shook his head. "There's no turning back." He pointed at the road. "Look. There isn't room to turn around. We'll have to go wherever this takes us."

"Then slow down at least!"

Luke didn't seem to hear her. He kept driving, faster and faster, tightly cornering each hairpin bend. Sarah imagined herself in the film, *Thelma and Louise*, making a suicide run into the Grand Canyon. Fifty metres beneath them was the hollow full of rubble. It looked like a death pit.

"If you don't slow down," she yelled at Luke,

"I'll, I'll . . ." Before she could work out what she meant to say, Sarah screamed, as the next bend revealed a huge rock blocking their path.

They were driving straight into it.

Luke did an emergency stop. For a moment, Sarah thought they were going to skid off the track. But the car came to a juddering halt against the rock instead. The bumper was bent, but the car's two occupants were unharmed.

"Damn!" Luke said. "We'll have to move it."

Tears flooded down Sarah's face. She was shocked and relieved to be safe.

"Don't . . ." she began to beat her fists against Luke's chest. "Don't ever do anything like that to me again."

Luke put his arm around her. "Calm down, baby, calm down. You were never in any danger. Trust me."

"I want to trust you!" Sarah yelled. "But you're making it really, really hard."

"Come on," said Luke, getting out of the car. "Let's shift this rock."

This was easier said than done. The rock was half Sarah's height and very heavy. Moreover, it was deeply embedded in the ground.

"Mark must have come down a different way," Luke muttered on their third attempt.

"Isn't there any way we can lever it? Does the car have a wheel brace?"

"One of those things that turns the jack? Let's look."

They found the wheel brace in the boot. After a lot of prodding and pushing, they managed to wedge it in a gap beneath the rock. Then the two of them put all their weight onto the metal rod. Slowly, the rock began to move.

"Back!" Luke yelled.

The rock picked up momentum, moving forward as the couple pressed their bodies against the cliff wall. The movement of the rock had started a small landslide, but nothing hit them. There was a huge crashing sound. When they looked over the edge, the rock was gone, smashed into smaller stones scattered around the rubble.

"Let's hope we don't get a puncture," Luke said, picking up the mangled wheel brace, which was even more badly bent than the bumper.

"Where do you want to go now?" he asked, as they set off again, this time at a more moderate speed.

"Just get us out of here," Sarah said, "and take me back to the hotel."

14

Brett Johnson was holding court by the hotel pool. He didn't like giving interviews, but Leo had insisted that he do some publicity for the film while he was in Britain. So the BBC's *Filmnight* was doing one of their "On Location" reports and a handful of journalists were getting a short press conference.

The TV people wanted the pool to look natural, so the director had asked members of the crew to hang around in their bathing costumes. Jon had nothing better to do. Neither had Mary. She was excited about having got the small part of the model/bridesmaid, which hadn't been in the original script, and hoped to get her picture in the TV report.

"*This Year's Model* is turning into my big break," she told Jon. "My agent says I'll get lots of offers if it's a hit."

"I'm sure you will."

"Tell me, Brett, why did you choose this picture for your comeback?" asked the *Filmnight* presenter.

"It was the script," Brett said with a twinkle in his eye. "It's an original variation on a strong theme. And the director, of course. I've been following Leo's work for a long time now."

The presenter leaned forward with a nervousness that implied he was going to ask a "difficult" question.

"You're working with Luke Kelly for the first time. Now, he's got the sort of reputation that you used to have: bit of a hell-raiser, demon with the ladies and – not to put it mildly – a nightmare to work with. How have you found him?"

Brett gave his sweetest smile. "Luke's a pussycat. I've heard those stories but, let me tell you, if he wants to get a reputation as bad as mine used to be, he's got one hell of a lot of work to do."

The presenter laughed sycophantically. "Now the one real surprise in the casting for this movie was the choice of Sarah Wood as the leading actress. Without spoiling the plot, is it true that you get to marry her during the film?"

Brett raised his eyebrows slightly. "There are wedding bells, yes. But something gets in the way of the wedding night. I won't tell you what that is, but I will tell you one thing: Sarah's had no acting experience, but Leo knew exactly what he was doing when he cast her for this movie. She's a natural. It wouldn't surprise me if she won an Oscar before she's twenty-one."

"Praise indeed," the presenter said. "Let me finish with a . . . sensitive question. It's ten years since you won your own Oscar for best actor and four since you last made a film. Do you think you can make it all the way back, to become as successful as you were before?"

Brett shrugged and smiled enigmatically. "Others have done it. Look at Richard Gere. Heck, look at Dennis Hopper. But, to be honest, I don't think about it much. I guess I just feel lucky to have survived. I've lost some friends along the way. I feel like I owe it to them, and to my fans, to do the best I can."

"Brett Johnson, thank you very much."

There was a screeching noise as a car pulled up in the car park.

"Mr Fitzgerald, can you come over here for your interview?" one of the BBC production assistants asked.

"Wait a minute."

Fitzgerald shot off towards the car park. Jon got out of the pool. He could see why Leo had hurried off the moment he saw the car – it was Fitzgerald's own. Sarah got out of it. Ignoring the director, she marched straight to the hotel entrance.

Fitzgerald pointed angrily at the bumper of the car, which was dented. He and Luke had a heated argument. Jon considered getting closer, finding out what was going on, but decided against. He walked back to the pool. Should he go to Sarah? No. She'd find him if she needed him. Jon wondered if, by showing her the newspaper article, he'd caused a row between her and Luke.

The BBC crew were getting some pool shots. Mary was preening herself enthusiastically. Jon jumped into the water, dive-bombing her. Why shouldn't he have some laughs for a change? Mary retaliated by throwing a beach ball at him. For a few minutes they managed to have some silly, childish fun.

"Jon!" Leo Fitzgerald had returned to the set. "The BBC are keen on getting a couple of minutes with your sister. Could you fetch her?"

"I'm wet," Jon told him. "Can't you phone her room?"

Fitzgerald shook his head. "She's not answering. I think she's in a bad mood. She might need some persuading. Get her down here, will you? What do you think I pay you for?"

Resentfully, Jon got out of the pool. He was an extra, a gofer, and, yesterday, a temporary camera assistant, but Fitzgerald wouldn't let him forget that he'd got the job because he was Sarah Wood's brother.

He knocked on her door.

"Who is it?"

"Jon."

"Go away. I don't want to see anybody."

"Leo sent me. They need you to answer a couple of questions for this BBC thing."

"I won't do it."

"Fine, I'll tell him. But Sarah, what's wrong?"

There was no reply, but as he pressed his ear to the door, Jon could make out a whimpering sound. She was crying.

"Sarah, please let me in. I want to help. Let me in."

A few moments later, the door opened. His sister's face was red and blotchy.

"He dumped you, did he?"

She shook her head. "No. I dumped him. But it feels just as bad as if he did it."

"What happened?"

Sitting on her bed, Sarah told Jon about her day.

"First there was that awful newspaper story. Then there was the horrible row with this pathetic boy in the car park."

As she told him the story, Jon felt a stab of recognition.

"That was Slacker."

"You know him?"

"Not really. I thought he actually had a job on the set. He must have been pretending."

"Pretending?"

"Yeah. He was desperate enough. First the kid pretended to be an extra, then he must have borrowed the fire guard equipment. That explains why he disappeared so quickly afterwards."

"Fire guard?" Sarah asked, confused.

"Yes," Jon told her. "Didn't you realize who he was?"

From the blankness in Sarah's face, it was obvious that she didn't. "What do you mean?"

"What I mean is, he's the guy who pulled you out of the fire yesterday. He might have saved your life."

"Oh, no!" Sarah said. "And I helped them get rid of him."

"It sounds to me like you tried to help him."

"But I should have helped him more. I should have . . ." Sarah looked mortified.

"What happened next?" Jon prompted.

Sarah told him about a horrifying drive around a dangerous, deserted quarry and an ice-cold, silent journey back. Then she became more tearful.

"And the nearer to the hotel I got the more I thought, *I can't go to America with this bloke. I can't introduce him to Mum and Dad.* He's six or seven years older than me, but he acts like a spoilt child and he treats me like I'm there purely for his amusement."

"At least you worked it out in time." Jon gave Sarah a big hug.

"But I fell in love with him," she cried. "I've never been in love before. I've had crushes, but they didn't mean any more than sticking some film star's picture on the wardrobe door."

"Mum took those pictures down," Jon told her. "They'd started to fade. The sellotape was peeling."

Sarah laughed bitterly. Then she pulled away from Jon and looked him straight in the eye.

"I wasn't in love, was I?" she said. "I just wanted to be. I turned a blind eye to his faults. I was in love with the idea of being in love with Luke Kelly."

"But you're not any more."

"No, I'm not."

There was a knock at the door.

"Sarah, it's Leo. The BBC are waiting downstairs."

"I'll get rid of him," Jon told her.

"No. I've got a bone to pick with him."

She opened the door and raised her voice. "If you think I'm going anywhere near the press after that story this morning, you've got another think coming. Or maybe I will. Maybe I'll tell them the real story of how you nearly got me burnt to death yesterday!"

"Both those things were Luke's idea," Fitzgerald

protested. His voice was urgent. "Please let me explain."

Reluctantly, Sarah left the door open.

"You think I want to publicize accidents on my set? Luke suggested that we let the thing build up a bit more before he went in. Maybe he added some petrol. If he did, I don't know where it came from or what happened to it. Anyway, I'm sorry. I guess we overdid the effects. Luke wanted to stage this dramatic rescue and persuaded me that it would make terrific publicity. But somehow the fire got out of control. I had to drag him out. You were never in any serious danger."

"It felt like it."

"Brett was the one who nearly suffocated."

"He didn't have to go straight on and film another scene an hour's drive away."

"OK," Leo admitted "Maybe I was over-zealous about that, but we'd never have got that look with make-up, and Luke was keen."

"You're the director," Jon cut in. "You're responsible, not Luke."

"No one was hurt," Leo insisted. "We got the publicity. We got some magnificent footage. I looked at the rushes last night. We've got some terrific reaction shots on Sarah."

"So that's what this is all about," Sarah said. "You still think that I can't act, so you had to make it real."

Fitzgerald shook his head. "Brett was just telling the BBC you're a natural. And you get better the more we go on. But every actor needs a little goading now and then, a little danger. It's the way I work."

"Well I don't like it!" Sarah said, slamming the door on him.

"Just wait till I get my hands on Luke Kelly," Sarah said to Jon. "He'll wish he never left Hollywood."

"Do you think he set up that other thing as well?" Jon asked. "The exploding motor boat?"

"I don't know," Sarah said. "But I intend to find out. There's nothing I'd put past him."

15

The phone rang just after Jon had left the room. Sarah was trying to sleep, but couldn't get thoughts of Luke out of her mind. Half of her hoped that this would be him. But it wasn't. It was her agent, Sally.

"I've had Leo Fitzgerald on the phone. He says that you're refusing to do interviews and you're in a mess over Luke Kelly." Sally's voice softened. "I thought I'd better see if you were all right, Sarah. Are you?"

Sarah told her what had happened since they last spoke. Sally was sympathetic but business-like.

"Directors have to be dictatorial. They're in charge of huge budgets. But I'll relay your safety concerns to the studio. In the meantime, though, don't forget that Leo is giving you a big break. And your contract does specify that you'll be available for publicity whenever practicable."

"It's a rest day," Sarah argued.

"It's free publicity, for you as well as the film. Put on your prettiest frock. Put Luke Kelly to the back of your mind. Please."

"OK, Sally, but for you, not for Leo Fitzgerald."

"Thank you, dear."

Sarah put on her favourite white linen dress, made herself up, then chose a pair of blue sunglasses. Her eyes were still puffy from crying. As she was about to leave, the phone rang. She nearly didn't answer it. After all, if it was Luke, she had nothing to say to him. Once she made up her mind about something, she never changed it.

It was Luke. He sounded distraught.

"I just wanted to say . . ."

"Don't say anything," she interrupted. "It's over."

She hung up.

Acting in front of a camera was one thing. Being interviewed by a TV presenter whose show she always watched was another. Sarah wished that she was in the pool, not sitting by it in the bright sunshine. She tried to relax, but nearly froze up completely once the questions started.

"Sarah, you've had amazing success as a model

just recently, but now you're starting a movie career. Why the sudden transition?"

Sarah smiled awkwardly at the presenter, trying to look glamorous and modest at the same time.

"Leo made me an offer I couldn't refuse. When I went to see him I thought that the part would be just a cameo, but he had amazing faith in me. And I couldn't turn down the opportunity to work with Brett, who's always been one of my favourite actors."

This wasn't strictly true. You had to varnish the facts in situations like this. But there was a limit. Sarah wasn't going to praise Luke if she could avoid it. The presenter asked her a question about her role, which she answered in detail.

". . . so, in a sense, I'm playing myself, but I hope to take on more varied and challenging parts in the future."

"Does that mean your modelling days are over?"

Sarah gave him a big, bashful smile. "Oh, I'm not ready to give up my day job just yet. We'll see."

The presenter leant forward and brushed her arm in what was meant to be a sensitive gesture. "There's one other question which I have to ask you, because if I don't, the tabloid reporters who've been hanging around all day will. I don't mean to pry but . . . are there real-life wedding bells for you and your co-star Luke Kelly?"

Sarah lost her cool.

"That's ridiculous! Who told you that? Was it Leo?"

The presenter prevaricated.

"Well, er . . . there have been all these rumours . . . the story about him rescuing you from a fire . . ."

Sarah spoke sternly.

"They're all rubbish. My relationship with Luke Kelly is purely professional. Any other story is just publicity."

The presenter laughed nervously.

"It sounds as though you don't like him very much."

"I don't know Luke Kelly very well," Sarah said straight into the TV camera, "but my impression of him so far is that he's mad, bad and dangerous to know. Does that answer your question?"

"It does. Sarah Wood, thank you very much for joining me."

"You're welcome. I'm sorry I kept you waiting."

As Sarah walked back to the hotel, half a dozen reporters ran up to her, blocking her path.

"Sarah, if we could have a comment or two."

She snapped back.

"Did you hear what I just told the BBC?"

"Yes, but . . ."

"Then I'm sorry, but I've got nothing to add."

"Aw, c'mon. Nothing?"

She marched into the lobby with the hacks following her.

"Luke! There you are," one of them called out. "Could we have a few words?"

Sarah looked round, just in time to see her brother saying, "I'm not Luke Kelly."

He walked over to Sarah. "How did it go?"

"All right. But I'd like to get away from these bloodsuckers."

"I've got my car," Jon told her. "We could drive somewhere."

"Why not? I don't want to spend any more time in my room."

As they walked back outside again, Sarah heard shouts.

"There they are! Get them!"

Cameras clicked. Jon and Sarah ignored them.

"I can see the stories now," Jon said. "*Sarah consoles herself with mystery Luke look-alike.*"

"With any luck," Sarah told him, "someone will tell them who you are and they'll figure that the rumours about me and Luke were the result of people confusing the two of you."

Jon shook his head.

"They'll print whatever suits them," he said, "whatever sells the most papers. You should know that by now."

"Yes," said Sarah. "I guess I should."

They drove out in the direction that Luke had taken Sarah before.

"There's a good pub in a village about fifteen kilometres away," Jon told her. "They do decent food and it's pretty quiet."

They had a peaceful lunch, sitting outside at a wooden table by a stream. No one recognized Sarah. No one confused Jon with Luke Kelly. Jon made light conversation, avoiding the subject of the American actor. Later, perhaps, they would confront Luke about the fire, about whether the time he saved Sarah's life had been faked, too. But that could wait. Now, the pair of them talked about family and old friends.

Sarah was aware that she had grown apart from her brother over the last few months. Her relationship with Luke hadn't helped either. But now the distance between them seemed to melt away. It was like old times. Sarah filled Jon in on films she'd seen in the States which hadn't reached Britain yet. Jon told Sarah about things on television that she'd missed.

By the time the pub was throwing out, Sarah had loosened up a lot.

"Will you make more films?" Jon asked her.

"I hope so. I've enjoyed this one a lot. Sally's already looking for another part for me, but she says that I probably won't get really good offers until *This Year's Model* comes out."

"If it's any good."

Sarah nodded. "A big *if*. How about you?" she added. "Has doing the film given you any ideas?"

Jon grinned. "I'd really like to make films," he said. "The life suits me. The work fascinates me. But I still want to go to university," he added. "I've learnt a lot these last few weeks and maybe the experience would help me get a job. But I don't want to go straight into a career just yet. I want time to think, mess around, maybe make a few experimental videos or films on Super-8. Of course I might not get into university . . ."

"When are the results out?"

"This Thursday. If I do get in, I'll probably concentrate on the Media side of the degree."

One of the bar staff started ostentatiously wiping down the table next to them.

"Come on," Jon said. "Let's go."

He drove Sarah back to the hotel by a different route, for variety. As they got nearer to the hotel, Sarah began to look disturbed.

"What is it?"

"Oh, nothing. This bit up ahead, I think it's where Luke took me earlier."

"Sorry."

"It doesn't matter."

As she spoke, they saw that the road ahead of

them was blocked. There was already barely room for two cars to pass each other, but a police car appeared, braked sharply, and turned a narrow corner. There was an ambulance behind it. The white vehicle tried to follow the police car into the dirt road, but failed, getting one of its wheels stuck in a rut.

"We'd better help," Jon said.

He parked the Nova on the verge and he and Sarah walked over to the stranded ambulance.

"Need a hand?"

"Please," said the driver. "I hadn't realized how bad this track was."

With a bit of pushing they got the ambulance free and it backed onto the lane.

"Aren't you going up there?" Jon asked the driver.

"What? And risk that happening again? No. We'll wait here. It's just come over on the radio. There's very little chance of getting the body out."

"What happened?"

"There's an old quarry at the end of that track. It's meant to be sealed off but kids with motorbikes are always getting rid of the fences and going for a burn. Evidently someone went over the side."

"I see."

"Luke," Sarah said.

Jon turned round to see his sister looking distraught.

"I've got this feeling that it's Luke," she said.

"Why?" he asked her. "Is this the place he brought you to?"

"Yes. Jon, we must take a look."

Without another word, Jon went back to his car and drove it round the ambulance to the entrance.

"I'm sure you'll be wrong," he told Sarah as she got in. "It'll be some kid on a motorbike like the ambulance driver said."

"I expect you're right," Sarah said, looking distracted as they rattled along the road.

They drove in silence. There was a police car parked at the top of the road. Two police officers were talking to a youth with a motorbike. Presumably, he was the one who had reported the accident. Jon stopped his car and got out.

"What's going on?" he asked the first officer.

"There's been an accident. I'd rather you left, sir. This is private land and we don't need spectators."

"We're not spectators," Sarah said. "We came up here because we're worried about a . . . a colleague of ours. Who's been hurt?"

"Hard to tell," said the officer, pointing into the quarry. "Whoever it was is nearly covered up now."

Jon looked over the side. He could see nothing – just endless rubble, piled at the bottom of a sheer drop.

"There used to be a way through to there," the second officer told them, "but there've been so many landslides it would take a week to dig our way in."

"Not that there's any chance of the person in the car still being alive," the first officer said. "Not after that fall, and the fire."

"Car?" Sarah interrupted. "Did you say it wasn't a motorbike, it was a car?"

"I saw it go over," the lad in the motorbike jacket told her. "Whoever it was was driving like a maniac, really fast."

"What was he driving?" Jon asked.

The motorcyclist told him.

"It was one of them vintage sports cars – don't know the name," the motorcyclist said. "Red, it was. Just went flying off the road, landed with a big bang. Then the tank must have gone up because it caught fire. Probably died quickly. Better than the other way."

"What other way?"

"Buried alive. After the car crashed, what with all the vibrations, there was a big landslide. The wreckage must be fifteen metres under by now."

Sarah's face had turned a deathly pale.

"Do you know who was inside the car, miss?" the first officer asked.

"Yes," said Sarah. "I was here with him earlier today. He's an American actor. His name's Luke Kelly."

16

The press conference was called for seven that evening. Leo wore a black suit. He also had black sunglasses on, even though the briefing was taking place in one of the hotel conference rooms. He spoke into a microphone.

"Luke Kelly died at between three and four this afternoon. His death was a tragic accident. I, the studio and everyone involved in the production of *This Year's Model* would like to pass on our deepest sympathy and condolences to his family." He paused. "And now the Detective Inspector and I will answer any questions you have."

"How exactly did it happen?" a reporter asked the Inspector.

"The information we have so far suggests that

Mr Kelly drove off a narrow quarry road and his car – I should say the car that he borrowed from Mr Fitzgerald here – fell over fifty metres. In such circumstances, death would almost certainly have been instantaneous."

"Have you recovered the body?"

"That may take some time."

"Is there any chance that he's still alive?"

"None whatsoever."

"What about suicide?" a woman from the *Daily Mail* asked. "Could he have done it deliberately?"

The Inspector shook her head.

"We have an eyewitness. As far as the police are concerned at this stage, there are no suspicious circumstances."

"Mr Fitzgerald, would you care to comment on Luke's relationship with the model, Sarah Wood?"

Watching from the back of the room, Sarah flinched.

"No, I would not. And Miss Wood is not answering any questions today."

"Was Luke insured, Mr Fitzgerald?"

"We always insure our stars," Fitzgerald announced confidently, "but it's unlikely that we'll need to claim on our policy. Practically all of Luke's performance is already in the can."

Surely that can't be true, Sarah thought. As far as she knew, the film's ending still hadn't been definitively worked out, never mind shot. How could they have an ending without Luke?

"How long will you be suspending production for, Mr Fitzgerald?"

The director didn't pause for breath. "We won't. Luke was an important young actor, but I knew him well, and he wouldn't have wanted us to stop work for even one minute. We're on a tight schedule. We'll be completing the shoot this week and the film will be on general release by Christmas. It's the way I work. It's the way Luke would have wanted it. This is his last picture. We hope to make it his best." He stood up. "That's all, folks."

There was a barrage of questions, but Fitzgerald ignored them. Sarah slipped out quietly before the reporters' insatiable curiosity could be turned on her. She felt tormented. If she hadn't finished with Luke . . . if she had just spoken to him on the phone, maybe he wouldn't have done something so reckless. Did he mean to kill himself? She would never know. But she would always feel directly responsible for his death.

"Jon, I want a word . . . alone."

Jon followed Leo Fitzgerald up to his suite. It was a massive, luxurious room, with a computer and printer in one corner and a wide-screen TV and video in the other. There were multi-coloured sheets of paper everywhere. He had no idea what the director wanted.

"Drink?"

Leo opened the fridge, which was filled with bottled beers and wines. Jon asked for a Pilsner Urquell.

"You look like Luke," Fitzgerald said as he poured the beer into a glass.

"A little," Jon agreed.

"A lot," Fitzgerald insisted, "from a distance. We can make your hair identical. And if we shoot you in profile, in shadow, no one will be able to tell the difference."

Jon couldn't believe his ears. "You want me to *be* Luke Kelly? What about my voice? I'm not a mimic."

"Don't worry about that," Fitzgerald told him. "We'll get someone convincing to dub the voice when we're back in L.A. Will you do it?"

Jon thought about it. "Didn't you just tell the press conference that practically all of Luke's part had already been shot?"

Fitzgerald smiled ruefully. "I was lying. The last thing we want is for the public to realize that they're not watching the real Luke Kelly. We've got a love scene and the climax to do. We'll need you for three days' shooting on a closed, high-security set. Are you in?"

It was obvious that Fitzgerald really needed Jon.

It seemed a mercenary thing to do, but Jon decided to be hard-nosed about the deal.

"How much extra will you pay me?"

Fitzgerald smiled as though he'd been expecting the question.

"We can't do this through the books. The unions would have a fit. I'll put you down on incidental expenses. Two thousand pounds, in your back pocket."

"Five."

The director kept a poker face. "All right," he said finally, "three."

Jon shook his head. "Split it down the middle."

"OK, four." Fitzgerald sighed. "That's a lot of money for an eighteen-year-old."

Jon smiled and shook his hand. "Maybe I'll use it to finance my first film."

Fitzgerald laughed unconvincingly. "See Debbie, the production accountant. She'll give you half tomorrow and half when you've finished. Now remember, absolute secrecy on this. Only the people who are directly involved in the production need to know about it."

"OK," said Jon. They shook hands.

"You'd better learn this," Fitzgerald told him, thrusting a computer print-out into Jon's hands. "I've just rewritten it to avoid having to shoot any close-ups. Your lines are marked."

Jon went back to his room and read the pages.

Who would die at the end? Brett, as in one version? Or Luke, as in another? At last he would get to find out.

Sarah looked at herself in the mirror. It was the morning after Luke's death and she felt haggard. At seventeen, she looked thirty-five. It would take Make-up a lot of time to get her halfway presentable. The show had to go on, Leo Fitzgerald said, and she had to fulfil her contract. But the last thing she felt like filming was a love scene, body double, or no body double.

There was a knock on her door. She hoped that it was Jon. He had comforted her the previous afternoon, but she hadn't spoken to him since the press conference to announce Luke's death. When she'd called his room, Todd had been evasive about Jon's whereabouts.

"Come in," she called.

Jon was an enigma to her. Until yesterday afternoon, he'd behaved so coldly during the shoot, Sarah had half suspected him of being behind one of the odd accidents which had plagued them. She hated the way he looked at her sometimes, like she wasn't his sister, but some kind of object.

No one opened the door, so Sarah got up and opened it herself. It wasn't Jon. He would have just barged in, not waiting for her to reply. It was Brett. The actor was holding a bunch of white lilies.

"I thought you might appreciate someone to talk to," he told her.

"Thanks," she said, taking the flowers. "It was nice of you to come."

"You've got a pretty bad press this morning," Brett said. "I thought someone ought to warn you."

"It's OK," Sarah said. "I'm expecting it."

"You think you are," Brett told her, "but when the vilification starts to hit you, it'll hurt. I know. I've been there."

Sarah remembered various rumours about Brett's past.

"I know what it's like to be responsible for someone's death," Brett told her.

"You do?"

He nodded. "A girl I was dating, not much older than you. I was a wreck at the time, out of my head on drugs and booze. I was driving her to the beach. I went off the road, turned the car over. I got out of the car without a scratch on me. She broke her neck. There isn't a day goes by that I don't think about that girl and her family."

"It's good of you to confide in me," Sarah told him, "but you're not making me feel any better."

Brett smiled sincerely. It was odd, being here alone with him. It didn't feel real. His expression was so familiar, Sarah felt like she was watching him in a movie.

"The point I'm trying to make," Brett said, "is that I was responsible for that girl's death. But you aren't responsible for Luke's. He killed himself, deliberately or otherwise."

"If it hadn't been for me . . ." Sarah began to say.

Brett shook his head. "It might still have happened the same way. Luke was a reckless young man who found it hard to handle fame. His career had hit a plateau and he knew that the only place for him to go from there on was down. Maybe he decided that it was better to be a dead legend than a live has-been."

"You think so?"

"I do. There've been times when I've considered that course myself." He leant forward. "Listen to me, Sarah. Luke was talented but, from what I've seen, you have the promise to be a more mature actor than he was. You're already a more mature person. Don't let his death drag you down too."

There was a call from outside.

"Sarah, are you ready?"

"Coming."

She stood up and kissed Brett on the forehead.

"Thanks," she told him. "You helped."

When Sarah walked onto the set, she thought she was seeing a ghost.

". . . Luke?"

For a moment, she thought she was going to faint, but then she heard her brother's voice.

"Didn't anybody warn you?"

"You're pretending to be Luke?"

"That's right."

She turned to Leo Fitzgerald. "Does that mean we still have to do the love scene?"

"That's right."

"So where's my body double?"

Fitzgerald looked irritated. "What do you mean?"

"I told you before that I'm not going to take my clothes off. Sally said she'd sorted it out with you. I haven't changed my mind."

"We can't have both people in a love scene played by body doubles," Leo protested, "it wouldn't work."

"That's your problem," Sarah told him.

Fitzgerald threw his hands in the air. "All right, I give in. Let's drop it. Luke was the one who was really keen on the nudity anyway."

Sarah was flabbergasted. "It was *Luke's* idea?"

"That's right. He said that steamy sex scenes were important to his new image."

"Now are you convinced that he was a prat?" Jon whispered.

"Yes," Sarah muttered back. "I think I am."

"OK," said Fitzgerald. "Jon, get down to your shorts. Sarah, put your nightie on. Let's get on with this."

They both changed and got into bed. It felt ridiculous.

"Oh, Aidan," said Sarah. "How could I have been so wrong about you?"

"It's not your fault," Jon replied, in a flat monotone. "Anyway, we're together now. I love you."

"And I love you too . . ."

As Brett burst into the room, interrupting them *in flagrante*, both Jon and Sarah burst into hysterical laughter.

"Cut!"

"I'm sorry," said Sarah, still giggling, as she let out all the tension of the weekend. "This might take some time."

17

"Are the rumours true?" Mary asked Jon as he sat down for his lunch. "Are you doubling for Luke?"

"My lips are sealed."

"I'll bet they are!"

She planted a kiss on them. Suddenly, after flirting with Jon for nearly six weeks, she was making a play for him. Jon was flattered, but he wasn't interested. These days he was too concerned with acting and his sister's safety to get involved in a romance.

"What are you doing tonight?" she asked.

"I'm busy," he told her with a grin. "I've got lines to learn."

"Some other time maybe."

"Maybe."

She got up to go, looking hurt. She wasn't used to being given the brush-off.

"Oh," she said, trying to sound casual but with an edge to her voice. "Have you seen the papers?"

"Only *The Guardian*."

"Congratulations!" she said bitchily. "You made the front page of both the *Mirror* and *The Sun*."

Mary pulled a paper out of her bag, handed it to Jon, and walked off.

"THE GIRL WHO DROVE LUKE KELLY TO HIS DEATH" was the headline. Beneath it was a photograph of Sarah and Jon, walking into the hotel two days before. The caption said that the photo was of "*Luke with supermodel Sarah, only hours before his death. A few minutes after this photograph was taken, she dumped him.*"

"What?" Jon said aloud.

The story was worse.

Superstar Luke Kelly took his own life after being rejected by haughty supermodel Sarah Wood, friends believe. Luke had told them that Sarah was "the love of his life," but she dumped him after a tempestuous, month-long romance. "She was just playing with his affections," a close colleague said, "and when he got too serious she dropped him like a hot brick. Luke was heartbroken."

The police will not say whether Luke's death was accidental or suicide, and the inquest may be delayed because of difficulties excavating the quarry where Luke met his tragic death. He and Sarah had visited it only hours before in the car which he would die in. Psychologists say that the manner of his death was almost certainly a message to Sarah. Miss Wood was unavailable for comment last night.

Meanwhile, fans all over the world have been mourning the superstar's death.

"It's unbelievable!" Jon said to Todd, who was sitting by him. "They're vilifying her!"

"That's just the press," Todd replied. "Wait until some of Luke's fans get anywhere near Sarah. They're bound to blame her for his death. If I were her, I'd get a bodyguard for the next year or two."

The days immediately after Luke's death were the worst. The production was constantly plagued by the press. Sarah couldn't see Jon, except on the closed set, in case his role leaked to the media. The story still hadn't died down. On the breakfast news, there had been an item about how police had had to abandon attempts to dig out Luke's body because of the danger. There'd been another landslide.

Sarah was upset about Luke's death and still blamed herself, but there was no one she could really talk to about it. Jon was too biased against

Luke. Her parents were too far away. And her part in *This Year's Model*, which was meant to boost her career, was having the opposite effect. In the few days since his death, Luke's legend had grown and grown. Teenage girls held endless wakes. Actors who had refused to work with him in the past saluted his "great talent". There was talk of a posthumous Oscar. His death was romantic – attributed not to drink or drugs but to a broken heart. And Sarah was the one who broke it. She was Public Enemy Number One. She had no movie future and the papers now described her as an "ex-supermodel". Sally rang to say that there had been several cancellations.

"Adverts that are meant to appeal to young women, basically," Sally explained. "Obviously they can't risk alienating the Luke Kelly audience while you're cast as the villain of the piece."

"I see," Sarah replied. "Have there been any new offers?"

"Only the kind that you don't like me to pass on to you," Sally told her. "Men's magazines, that kind of thing. Don't worry. It'll all come out in the wash."

But Sarah knew it would take a long time to revamp her image. She'd had an incredibly success-ful year, but now it looked like it was all ending. Maybe it was for the best. Whatever talent she had wasn't worth the fantastic sums she earned. She was being paid for the way she looked, that was the sum of it.

And her looks were all that Luke Kelly had fallen for: a sexy waif with an English accent. Sarah wanted to be more than that. She wanted relationships that were more than skin deep. She wouldn't find what she was looking for in the fashion world, nor in motion pictures, that was for sure. Maybe she ought to welcome the end of her success. Maybe it was time for her to move on.

Since Luke's death, security had really tightened up. There was no chance of someone like Slacker hanging around the set now. Two of the guards even carried guns. The large men assured Sarah that this was to make her absolutely secure, but she wasn't convinced. Having guns around made her feel more at risk.

Every day there were reporters hanging around Bradlington Hall. Today, Sarah also noticed several young women, about her own age. They were wearing *Luke Kelly – the legend lives* T-shirts. When they saw Sarah coming, the women hissed. One of them shouted: "Murderess! Killer!"

Then there were other obscenities and threats. Sarah kept her head down. She felt terrible. In a way, she wanted to go over to them and explain, but anything she said would probably make things worse.

*   *   *

Sarah walked onto the set, script in hand, and greeted Jon. Finally the truth was to be revealed. Which of the men was the monster: the father or the son? Sarah knew the answer which was in the script, but she wouldn't be surprised if Fitzgerald changed it at the last moment. As she prepared, she could see the director and Brett, talking intensely.

"You ready?" she asked her brother.

"Ready as I'll ever be."

"All right," called Fitzgerald. "Let's go for it."

Sarah stood in the doorway, just behind a full-length mirror. Melissa was watching Matthew prepare the poison which was to kill her. He had been evil all along, while Aidan was in the right. Now, Matthew thought that his son was out of the way, and so did Melissa. But Aidan had secretly returned. In a moment Melissa, eavesdropping on her husband, would accidentally make a noise. Matthew would see her and realize that the game was up.

"OK, Sarah," Leo called. "Prepare to react as though your heel's suddenly snapped."

Sarah was meant to fall forward, in front of the mirror, but as she did, there was a commotion at the edge of the set. A teenage girl, not much younger than her, came running across the room screaming obscenities, pursued by a security guard.

Suddenly there was pandemonium. Several more young women followed the screaming girl. There were reporters close behind. Sarah flinched as the girl threw something at her. It landed on her chest. Then there was a flash like lightning. Sarah dropped to the ground, a red stain spreading across her chest.

"It's all right," Brett told Sarah, helping her up. "It's only tomato ketchup. They were setting you up for a photograph."

As Sarah looked around she saw Leo, wrestling with a photographer. A security guard grabbed the man from behind and Leo opened his camera, removing the film. "Get him out!" he shouted.

A minute later the other security guard returned and began apologizing to Leo. "All of a sudden there were so many of them. I think they were goaded on by some of the reporters. They made a run for it, with the press following. It won't happen again."

"It'd better not," Fitzgerald said, angrily. "Is everything clear?"

"We've got them all out. We're doubling the security presence at both entrances to the house."

"All right," said Fitzgerald. "Let's get on with it." He turned to the wardrobe manager. "Have we got another dress like that? We have to have her in the same dress for continuity."

"I'll get one."

Sarah got changed, feeling shaken. Even the men with guns hadn't made her any safer. Nor had she had one word of sympathy from the director. As soon as the film is over, she thought to herself, I'm going to get out of all this for a while. I'm not going to let them break me. I'll show everybody what I'm made of.

"Action!"

In her new dress, Melissa lurched out from behind the mirror. Matthew looked up. For a moment he looked alarmed, but then his suave, sneaky smiled returned.

"Hello, honey," he said. "I was just coming to look for you."

"I'll bet you were," Melissa told him.

"That's right," Matthew said, tipping the powder he'd been grinding into a glass of water. "I've made you a drink."

"Is that how you got rid of the others?" Melissa asked, with a sneer. "You poisoned them?"

"I've used it once before," Matthew admitted casually. "I made it look like heart failure."

"And the other deaths?"

"I arranged . . . accidents for them. However, in your case, the poison you'll be taking is very easy to detect. So, you see, I have to make it look like suicide."

"And how," Melissa asked, sardonically, "do you plan to do that?"

"Why," Matthew replied, "you're going to make it easy for me. You're going to sign this note."

He pointed to a sheet of paper sticking out of his typewriter. "Take it out," he said.

Melissa's body and her voice seemed to shake a little.

"What, and put my fingerprints on it? You must be joking."

Matthew shook his head. "No jokes. Take it out or I'll kill you with my bare hands." He grabbed Melissa and pulled her close to him. "Take it out!"

Without speaking, Melissa did as she was told. She read the note aloud.

"Matthew, my love,

I cannot live with my conscience any more. Now you know that I have been having an affair with Aidan, there is no hope for me. Aidan made me promises, but he has broken them. You were right about him all along. He's a liar and a cheat. I can't live with the ruin I've made of my life. Please forgive me, my darling. I won't be around to trouble you any more,

Your love,"

"Very sweet, the way you read that," Matthew told her. "Very convincing. Now sign it."

"You're joking!"

"No joke. Just write the one word, 'Melissa', underneath the word 'love'."

"And then you'll kill me?"

"Oh, no, my darling. Then you'll kill yourself. It'll be a quick death. And, believe me, the alternative is far more painful." He lifted her off her feet and pointed to the window. "The alternative is that I throw you out through that window. You'll probably be dead before you hit the ground, from fright."

"Like your third wife?"

"Precisely. Now sign it."

He put her down. Melissa picked up the pen, playing for time. She wrote her name very, very slowly as Matthew coaxed her.

"That's better. That's more like it. It'll all be over very quickly, I assure you."

They stood facing each other after she'd put the pen down.

"Satisfied?" she asked.

"Not yet," Matthew said. He picked up the drink. "I'll be satisfied when you've drunk this," he told her. She took the drink from his hands.

"Why?" she asked him. "Is it because of me and Aidan? Or were you always planning to do this?"

"I meant to do this all along," Matthew admitted, without any sign of guilt. "My son's involvement only made it happen sooner." He smiled, then added, "Don't worry. He's next. Now, drink."

Melissa lifted the glass to her lips while Matthew

continued to gloat. Then, with a quick jerking motion, she threw the drink all over his face.

Matthew took a step back, turning red with rage. "Young lady," he said, "you just made a big mistake."

"No," said Aidan, stepping into the room with a gun in his hand. "You're the one who made the mistake, Father!"

"Don't kill him!" Melissa shouted. "He's not worth it."

"Justifiable homicide," Aidan announced, pointing the gun. "The worst I'll get is a suspended sentence."

Matthew's face turned pale. Melissa waited awkwardly. The script called for Matthew to leap at Aidan just as he fired, making the shooting seem more justifiable. But it didn't work out that way. Just as Aidan squeezed the trigger, Matthew grabbed Melissa instead, pulling her in front of him.

Sarah didn't hear the gun go off. The next thing she felt was a searing pain across her chest and she was falling to the floor. There was a red patch spreading across her chest. Only this time it wasn't tomato ketchup. It was blood.

18

"Stupid move, sucker!" Matthew announced. "You won't get a suspended sentence for that."

"Cut!" Fitzgerald called. "Great work. I'm really glad we got that twist in. Sarah, you were superb. I'm sorry that I didn't warn you or Jon about the grab. I wanted a look of real surprise. Hey, Brett, did you have to burst such a big blood bag onto her?"

"It was a normal size one," Brett said.

"What I don't understand," Jon said to the director, "is what happens after this. I mean, it can't just end there, can it?"

The director tapped his nose with his finger.

"There might be a little more, but that's all I'm going to tell you. You'll have to wait until you see the final cut. Sorry, but I don't want any rumours leaking out."

"Killing the girl at the end is a brave move," Brett congratulated Leo. "A real anti-Hollywood ending. Do you think you can make it sell?"

"After what happened to Luke?" Fitzgerald said. "And with the way people feel about Sarah at the moment? They'll be cheering."

Jon felt angry at the way Fitzgerald had duped them. It seemed like the director was able to turn anything to his advantage. He walked over to his sister. There was still a pool of red liquid spreading around her. She hadn't got up.

"Sarah," he said, "are you all right? Sarah?" He leant over her. Blood was still pouring from her left breast. "Sarah?"

Her eyes flickered open for a moment but he could tell that she didn't really know what was going on. Jon began to yell.

"Get a doctor!" he screamed. "Call an ambulance! She's been shot! She's really been shot!"

19

Finally, the police let Jon go. He hurried to the hotel, where he changed and picked up his mail, then he took a taxi to the hospital. The surgeon who had operated on Sarah accompanied him down a corridor to the ward she was in.

"Your parents are already in there," she told him.

"Thanks."

"At least the press haven't got their hands on it," the surgeon went on. "The last thing your sister needs right now is to be hounded by the newspapers."

"Sure," Jon agreed.

It was funny, he thought, how Leo Fitzgerald could keep things out of the newspapers when he wanted to. Not a word had appeared about the accident which killed Karen either.

"Basically," the surgeon said, "it was a flesh wound. She lost a lot of blood and she needs time to rest and recuperate. Then she'll have a small scar, that's all."

"You're sure?"

"I'm sure. Now I'll leave you alone with your family."

She showed Jon into the room. Jon couldn't see his sister for the flowers which surrounded her. His parents stood up and greeted him. They hugged. Sarah smiled weakly. She was very pale. For once, she looked younger than her age.

"Hello," she said. "Sorry I can't get up to kiss you."

He embraced her.

"Did you get them?" she asked.

"What? Who?" He had no idea what she meant.

"Your 'A' level results. Did you get them?"

"Oh, that." He nodded. "An A and two Bs."

"That's brilliant!" Sarah said. "Congratulations."

Mum and Dad told him the same thing.

"How do you feel?" he asked Sarah.

"I'll survive," she sighed. "I guess this is one way of forcing myself to take a rest, decide what to do next. I've just been talking to Mum and Dad about it. I'm thinking of going back to school."

"Really?"

"Yeah. Why should you be the only one in the family to get a degree?" Sarah smiled weakly.

"Do they know what happened?" she asked.

Jon shook his head. "Not really. Somehow, the prop gun got switched with one belonging to a security guard. He left his holster in an office when they were chasing those girls who invaded the set. But no one can explain how they got switched. The police interviewed me for hours. I think they suspected me of wanting to kill you!"

"Where did you pick up the gun?" Sarah asked. "Didn't you notice that it was different?"

Jon shook his head. "As I told the police, I picked it up from a table by the door, just before I shot you. It was where it was meant to be. I took the safety catch off as I walked into the room."

"Could it have been an accident, a mix-up?" Mum asked.

"That's what Leo says, but I don't see how. The way I see it, someone switched those guns deliberately."

"But who?" Dad asked. "Who has a motive?"

Jon shrugged. "The police are trying to get hold of the fans who charged onto the set. They had it in for Sarah. But to switch guns, they'd have had to have known what was in the final script, which is more than I did."

"Can you think of anyone else who might have a motive?" Mum asked Sarah.

She thought for a minute. "The only person I can think of who'd consider doing a thing like that is Luke Kelly. And he's dead."

February

20

Unshaven, Jon got to the Arts faculty corridor at nine precisely and put his essay into Professor Cobain's pigeonhole. He had been up all night, but he had made the deadline. He had lectures to go to but he could borrow someone else's notes. All he wanted to do was get back to his Hall of Residence and catch some sleep.

Before going up to bed, he checked his own pigeonhole. There was an expensive-looking, cream-coloured envelope waiting for him. He took it up to his room and opened it.

You are invited to a charity premiere of a Leo Fitzgerald film, This Year's Model, *starring Brett Johnson and Luke Kelly in the presence of HRH* . . .

Jon threw the embossed invitation to the floor. It

annoyed him that the two men were listed as starring in the film, but Sarah wasn't. He got into bed. Should he go to the premiere? He wanted to see it, of course, but maybe he could wait until it showed up at the local cinema. He had no desire to meet members of the Royal Family. Then again, Sarah might want him there.

Jon's sister had changed since making the film. She had wound down her modelling career and was doing a one-year "A" level course in Drama and English Literature at the same college as many of the friends she went to school with. At first, it had been hard for Sarah. For a while there, Jon thought that she was on the verge of some kind of breakdown. She got a lot of press harassment. She took to wearing ugly glasses and baggy clothes so that editors were reluctant to publish photos of her. Then things loosened up. By the time she appeared in a college production of *Volpone*, a month ago, the press had totally lost interest in her.

Jon thought that Sarah was very good in the play. At Christmas, and at the party after the play, he'd been amazed by how relaxed she looked, and how ordinary. The aura of glamour which had descended on Sarah when she was barely a teen-ager had somehow been lifted. She looked much happier for it.

Jon was happy too. Working on *This Year's Model* had convinced him that he wanted a career in the film industry. He wanted to write screen-plays and, if possible, to direct them too. But it was a hard world to break into. There was no British film industry worth speaking of and he had only limited contacts. If he was going to get anywhere he'd have to work hard at it.

Already, he'd invested much of the money Leo gave him for doubling Luke Kelly in buying Super-8 film equipment. He'd started making a film featuring some student friends at weekends and during vacations. Hopefully, by the end of his course, he'd have a portfolio of work impressive enough to get him into the National Film School.

As Jon lay in his bed, trying to get to sleep, his mind whirred over the events of the previous summer. It had all been so dramatic, yet, looking back, he felt like he'd been an observer most of the time, like he was standing outside the action. But Jon often felt that way in life. Maybe that made him a natural writer/director. He noticed things that other people were too involved to pick up.

Sarah, when Jon last spoke to her about it, still thought that all the things which went wrong during the film shoot were accidents. Maybe, in her position, that was the only sensible thing *to* believe. Otherwise, she would still be worrying that someone was going to kill her at any moment.

But Jon wasn't so sure. After all, there had been five "accidents" during the making of the film. All but one – Luke Kelly's death – took place in suspicious circumstances. Jon figured that Luke had committed suicide as a way of getting back at Sarah. It showed how unbalanced the star was.

But that left four other "accidents", all of which could have killed his sister. OK, maybe some of them were coincidences, but *all four*? Jon resolved to go to the premiere if Sarah was going. The danger wouldn't be over until the killer was captured. At last he slept, dreaming of anonymous serial killers stepping out of enormous cinema screens.

Sarah didn't really want to go to the premiere, but it was for charity and she felt obliged. Once her health returned, she'd enjoyed being out of the public eye. And she'd applied to join RADA next year. She knew that if she wanted to be a good actress, she'd have to work hard at it.

Giving up modelling had been easy. All the bad publicity had cost her a lot of jobs. Anyway, since then the look had changed. No one wanted thin nymphets with flat chests any more. They wanted older, more full-bodied girls. Sarah didn't care. She'd made a load of money. She knew how little glamour there was in the fashion world. Now she wanted to get on with her real life.

Yet here she was, about to attend a press conference for *This Year's Model*, to be followed by a charity premiere that evening. Luke's death had created massive publicity for the film. A record number of prints had been made. In America, where it had been released two months ago, it was already a huge hit. But all the publicity had focused on Luke and his legend, not Sarah's performance.

Sarah ignored Leo Fitzgerald as she walked up the stairs to the table. Brett Johnson leant across and squeezed her hand. "You look great."

"I wish I didn't have to be here."

"Baptism of fire. You'll get used to it."

The conference began. Leo Fitzgerald gave a spiel about what a privilege it was that his film had been chosen for the charity event and pleaded with the press not to give away the movie's shock ending. Then Brett spoke about what a great privilege it was to work for Leo. He said he'd had a rough few years but now he was on the track to recovery. In response to a question he grinned and admitted that, yes, he was about to star in a major new TV series, but he wasn't at liberty to reveal the details just yet.

Then it was Sarah's turn.

She tried to keep her voice calm as she spoke into the microphone. But it was hard not to be aware of all the television cameras, to be conscious that millions of people across the world would be watching if she made a fool of herself. Sarah spoke briefly about what a big break the film had been for her and how she hoped eventually to have a career in acting.

"Wait until you see her performance," Brett broke in. "And you'll see that she doesn't have to hope. After this film, she'll be a major star."

Sarah smiled bashfully. "Thanks, Brett."

"We have time for a couple of questions," Leo said.

"Sarah," a woman from a TV news crew said, "now that you've had time to reflect on it, do you feel responsible in any way for Luke Kelly's death?"

"There's no need for her to answer that," Brett interrupted. "That's insulting."

"It's all right," Sarah said. "I'd like to answer it. My reply is: no, I am not responsible for what happened to Luke. It's true we argued that day, but I did not treat him badly – the reverse. I'm sorry about what happened, but we are all responsible for our own actions, and must take the consequences of them."

"Sarah, how have you dealt with the feelings of hate from Luke's fans? There's even a rumour that one of them *shot* you."

Sarah smiled sadly. "I'm not going to comment on rumours. And, as I said, I feel sorry about Luke and sorry for his fans. They want someone to lash out at. I can understand that. But I don't read the hate mail. It would be too upsetting."

"That's all we have time for from Sarah," Leo

announced. There was a shuffling noise as the media prepared to leave.

"But please don't turn your cameras or microphones off yet," the director pleaded. "Because we have a special surprise guest."

Sarah had no idea what the producer was talking about. They were bringing someone out from behind the curtain which served as a backdrop to the stage. There was an audible gasp.

"The fool!" Brett Johnson said, in a whisper loud enough for Sarah to hear. "A stroke like this might get him some cheap publicity, but it'll ruin his career at the same time."

Every reporter in the hall was yelling. Sarah looked around, curious to see who they had brought out. She was faced with a familiar, sickeningly smug grin. The object of everybody's attention walked towards her.

"You!" Sarah said, in a kind of hiss. Then she fainted.

21

Jon didn't usually watch television in the afternoon, but he was getting changed to go down to London for the premiere of his sister's film. He had rented a tuxedo from a costume hirer's and felt like a complete idiot.

He'd turn the set off in a minute, when children's programmes began, but in the meantime he might as well just take a look at the news headlines. For a while, in the summer, he'd not been aware of anything going on outside the tiny area of a film set. It was easy, he thought, for film people to think that they were the centre of the world, when all around them were wars, famine, corruption and other things which needed changing.

But today the main story wasn't about any of those things.

"Amazing scenes today at London's Metropolitan Hotel," the newsreader said, "as a film star literally returned from the dead. Luke Kelly, who co-starred alongside Brett Johnson in the new Warner's release *This Year's Model*, was thought to have died six months ago, when his car fell into a disused quarry. However, the body was never recovered, and today Kelly used the occasion of the British premiere of the film to announce his return. Mark Briggs reports."

The picture showed not Luke, but Sarah. She was talking at a press conference. However, the voice-over told another story.

"Luke Kelly's death was a secret which he kept from everybody. Even his ex-girlfriend, former supermodel Sarah Wood, was obviously in great shock."

The screen showed Sarah turning round, seeing Luke, and fainting.

"But Kelly, characteristically, made no apologies . . ."

The picture cut to Luke, dressed in black, smiling soberly as he faced the cameras. He spoke from a script.

"Films have been my whole life for five years now. It's difficult for me to exaggerate the pressures of stardom. This film, for various reasons, was very difficult for me. After it, I was due to return to the States to make another in a series of movies I

190

hated. I couldn't take the pressure any more. I wanted out and I took the only escape I could think of. I pretended to die."

"What about all the people you upset, Luke?"

Kelly glared at the camera.

"I made sure that the people who were closest to me knew what was going on. As for my fans – well, I'm grateful for their support, but I never asked them to make me some kind of a god. I'll understand if some of them feel let down by what I've done. But, you know, they don't know me, and they certainly don't own me. I did what I had to do."

"What exactly did you do, Luke? Where did you go?"

Luke smiled lugubriously.

"I went on a long journey – finding myself, if you like. I decided that I'd come back when I was ready. And now I am."

"Would it be fair to say that what you did was a stunt to get you out of a contract you hated and revive a fading career?"

"That's pathetic. I won't answer that."

A more enthusiastic voice shouted out, "Have you sold the film rights yet, Luke?"

He laughed and shook his head. "No, but as soon as we're through here, my agent will be very happy to deal with inquiries for the rights to *Vanishing Trick – The Luke Kelly Story*."

"Will you be at the premiere tonight?"

"I wouldn't miss it for anything. I'm a big fan of your Royal Family."

Jon noticed that Sarah and Brett had left the stage. Presumably they were as sickened by the whole thing as he was. On TV, even the newsreader looked a little disapproving.

"Tell me, Mark," she asked the reporter, "how has the film world reacted to the news of Luke Kelly's resurrection?"

"Well, Anna, a lot of people are saying that Kelly has gone just a bit too far this time. They're saying that the only role he's likely to pick up in the near future is that of Lord Lucan."

"Mark, thank you very much. And now the rest of the news . . ."

Two hours later, Jon spent nearly as long finding a parking place in the West End as it had taken him to drive there. He was meeting his sister inside. He wore his wire-rimmed spectacles, not wanting anyone to confuse him with Luke Kelly.

There was a throng of people outside the Warner West End, noisily waiting for the celebrities to arrive. Most of the people watching the film, however, would be ordinary punters who had paid a fortune for their charity ticket. Jon walked into Ruth who looked very different with her hair down. He'd read that she was about to make her first full feature. Ruth's boyfriend was a dark-haired man with a black beard. He was the man Jon had heard discussing Sarah's death with Leo in the trailer. The press collared him.

"Mr Costello, you wrote the original script for this film. Are you happy with the final cut?"

"I haven't seen it yet," the scriptwriter said, in a disenchanted tone. "I have no further comment."

No one said a word as Jon walked in himself, wishing that he hadn't had to wear a dinner jacket. To his surprise, Sarah was already in the cinema, waiting for him in their seats. She wore a striking, backless red dress.

"Why're you here so early?" he asked her.

"I wanted to avoid the crowds, and certain other people . . ."

"I understand. Mind you, now that Luke's alive, presumably your hate mail will stop."

Sarah grimaced.

"Presumably. But I wish that I could pay him back for all the grief he's caused me."

"You don't think . . ."

"What?"

Jon shook his head. "Nah, it's crazy. Only with him still being alive, I thought that maybe the shooting . . ."

Sarah finished the sentence for him.

". . . was Luke taking revenge on me? That's ridiculous. He's a spoilt, silly brat, but he's not that vindictive. No. I've convinced myself that all the odd things that happened on the shoot were just that – odd accidents. So please don't start up about it again. After tonight, I want to put everything to do with *This Year's Model* behind me."

"After tonight, you might be a star."

"*Please!* I haven't had any offers since it opened in the States. The reviews only mention me as a sinister sex object. My movie career was dead before it started."

Seats filled up. Jon spotted a familiar face.

"Yo, Slacker! You couldn't stay away, huh?"

The long-haired youth came over, smiling bashfully. It was odd to see him dressed in a jacket and tie.

"You're right," he said. "I couldn't resist seeing how it all turned out, though the ticket cost me an arm and a leg. What about Luke Kelly, eh? He sure had me fooled."

"Me too," said Sarah. "Look, I never got the chance to thank you . . . for what you did. I didn't find out about it until . . ."

"No sweat," Slacker told her. "You know, I was just hanging around, looking for some action. Anyone would have done what I did. I'm only glad that I managed to do something useful for once."

"Anyway," Sarah said, kissing him on the cheek, "thanks."

"You're welcome. Hey, aren't you meant to be meeting the Queen or something?"

"Oh, God!" said Sarah, checking her watch. "You're right."

Sarah got to the lobby in time to see Luke arriving, a beautiful, buxom starlet on his arm. Brett distracted Sarah.

"Don't look," he said. "He's not worth it."

Sarah smiled gracefully.

"You're right. I just want to make sure that I'm standing at the opposite end of the line from him."

"Come with me. I'll protect you. You know, you're looking particularly ravishing tonight. If I was twenty years younger . . ."

"You'd still be too old," Sarah told him.

Brett laughed.

"I like a woman who speaks her mind. Got any work lined up?"

Sarah shook her head.

"I've not looked. I'm thinking of going to drama school."

"Don't. Keep your talent fresh, untrained. The shadow's gone from your reputation now. You'll get lots of offers. Believe me."

They were interrupted.

"Mind if I stand between my two favourite stars?"

Sarah frowned at Leo Fitzgerald, but said nothing.

The Royals would be arriving at any minute. The hall was already quietening in anticipation.

"That was a stupid stunt, Leo," Brett muttered.

"Don't complain," Leo replied, under his breath. "It gave you the biggest hit of your career."

"At what cost?"

"Look," Leo hissed. "It wasn't my idea, but I went along with it. I'm annoyed with Luke, too. He was meant to hold back his reappearance until the film had had a full theatrical release. I think that he wanted to get back at Miss Goody Two Shoes here."

Sarah smiled. She was glad that she still had some power over Luke Kelly.

"But look at it this way," Fitzgerald went on. "You've got your TV series. Sarah's career will recover. The only person who'll suffer is Kelly. It's his funeral. Who's going to hire him after a debacle like this? He's committed commercial suicide."

"The witness," Sarah whispered, suddenly curious. "The motorcyclist. Did you pay him off?"

Fitzgerald nodded. "Luke did. The motorcyclist was an actor. The police won't be able to trace him. Mind you, they've already said that they want to interview Luke tomorrow. I hope he doesn't try to drag me into this. After all, I've already lost my favourite car."

There was a sudden hush as the Royal couple arrived. Sarah stood in line. Why was it, she wondered, that the Americans seemed more in awe of royalty than the Brits? When her turn came, she politely answered a question about modelling. Leo offered the Princess a role in his next film. Brett, however, got all tongue-tied. Then, mercifully, it was over. At last it was time to see the film.

22

Sarah slid into her seat next to Jon, then everyone had to stand up again as the Royal couple entered their box. Finally, the film began. The credits rolled, superimposed over the catwalk sequence, as Elvis Costello sang the title song. It was very sexy, very impressive. Sarah had avoided the cinema since making the film. She'd almost forgotten how mesmerizing an experience it could be.

The camera panned over the models on stage at the fashion show. As Prince sang "I wanna melt with you", the camera slowed down and zoomed in on Melissa. Sarah had seen herself in magazines and on television, but never like this: dressed to kill and two hundred feet tall. She didn't know how to react. The picture cut to Matthew.

"That one," he was saying. "The girl in yellow. I want her. What's her name?"

"Melissa. She's beautiful," the hard-looking woman next to him replied. "A little young maybe."

"I like them young. Get her on the country house shoot."

There was a short scene establishing Melissa, where she was offered the job at Matthew's friend's mansion. Then the film moved on to location. Bradlington Hall and the country surrounding it looked very different from the way Sarah had experienced it. She'd found the landscape boring, but on screen it looked quintessentially English. No wonder the Americans had lapped it up.

It was interesting for Jon to see it all on the big screen, slickly edited: Matthew's "accidental" meeting with Melissa (none of the fatal overhead shots were used) in the rain, then his careful seduction of her. Hitchcock would have done it better, Jon thought. He would have made Brett more sympathetic, more ambiguous. The way Leo had filmed it, you guessed that Matthew was a sleazeball from the start and the only issue was how corrupt he was. Had he actually killed his wives? And, if he had, would he do the same to Melissa?

The story unfolded. Sarah looked quite impressive, Jon thought, but it was hard for him to be objective about her performance or the film itself. Jon was too close to both. He knew exactly what was going to happen. The ballroom scene dragged, and the way in which Fitzgerald developed the relationship between Aidan and Melissa seemed laboured. But maybe that was because Jon disliked Luke so much.

Finally, it got to the parts Jon was most interested in seeing. The fire scene looked dazzling. On the score, the composer had used powerful gothic chords, like the ones Bernard Hermann used in *Psycho*, to build up the tension. The director kept cutting between Melissa trapped in her room and Aidan trying to get to her. Aidan knocked out his father in a fight, then you saw him battling his way through the flames. It annoyed Jon, though, to see Sarah in the role of weak victim, waiting to be saved. In real life, she hadn't panicked, as Luke had. She'd waited bravely until she didn't have the strength to escape.

In real life, Luke never actually got to Sarah, but the director got around this in a clever way. All you saw on the screen was a blazing inferno, but the music, along with Aidan's empassioned cries and coughs, convinced the viewer that he was still courageously fighting his way through the fire; that he got to Melissa; and, finally, that he was carrying her out of the building. At the end of the sequence, you saw Aidan and Melissa emerging into the daylight in their fire-damaged clothes. Aidan carried Melissa over his shoulder, then collapsed as soon as he was away from the burning house. It was very effective.

Jon was less convinced by the love scene. In the seat next to him, Sarah began to giggle. The pair of them had found it hard to keep a straight face while performing this very tame bed scene. The close-ups of Melissa showed the stress Sarah was under after Luke's death. For obvious reasons, there were no close-ups of Jon, until the very end of the scene, when, suddenly, Aidan stood up and walked over to a window to say his lines. Jon blinked. There were hairs on his chest where he didn't have any. Sarah poked him in the ribs.

"That's not you," she whispered. "That's Luke. Leo must have got him to film some pick-up shots in L.A. when he was in hiding."

That was Luke Kelly summed up, Jon thought: the actor couldn't resist taking his shirt off, even when he was supposed to be dead.

Sarah wasn't enjoying the film. She found watching her own performance excruciating. Everything on the screen reminded her of things she'd rather forget. However, she was curious to find out how it would end. She knew that she wasn't in it after the shooting, but didn't know what Fitzgerald had put in after that. The very end of the movie had been filmed in the studio, and Sarah wasn't needed. Her only involvement in the post-production process had been to dub a few lines of dialogue at a London studio.

The end was near. The film got to the part where Matthew was preparing the poison with which he meant to kill Melissa. The picture cut to Melissa, watching her husband from behind a full-length mirror. Sitting in the audience, Sarah didn't look at herself on the screen. She hated looking at herself. Instead, she focused on the mirror. To her surprise, she saw a fleeting image of somebody reflected there, somebody who wasn't supposed to be there. He had something in his hand. It looked like a gun.

Sarah froze in her seat. If this were a video, she could rewind it, make sure. But this was a Royal Command Performance. She remembered what had happened, how the filming of that sequence had been interrupted. There had been an invasion of irate fans. The person she thought she'd seen could have instigated it, could have sneaked in with them then, and switched the guns. Sarah began to feel scared. If what she saw was real, then that person really had tried to kill her. Her life was in danger. But that didn't make sense. Not unless . . .

Jon didn't notice his sister's distraction. He was anxious now to know how the film ended –

whether Fitzgerald had gone for the traditional happy ending or something more cynical. On screen, Jon saw himself shoot his sister, exactly as it had happened. Then there was Matthew's triumphant smile. It seemed that he had managed to kill two birds with one stone: Melissa was dead and Aidan would go to gaol for the killing. But surely the film couldn't end that way? Jon half expected Aidan to appear again, with the same gun. He expected to see Aidan blow Matthew's brains out.

Aidan did appear again, played by Luke Kelly. But he was standing behind the dock in a studio court room. The judge was saying:

"You have been found guilty of murder in the first degree. Your crime was a dreadful one, that of killing your own stepmother, and you have compounded that crime by your defence, in which you have slurred the reputation both of your stepmother and your own father. I have nothing but contempt for you, young man, and there is only one sentence suitable for you. That sentence is death."

Aidan looked in shock. The picture cut to Matthew, trying to suppress a smile.

Next to Jon, Sarah was trying to get his attention.

"It's important. We've got to get up, *now*!"

"Hold on," he whispered.

"Jon. Move!"

Sarah was standing, pushing her way along the

row. Reluctantly, Jon stood too, his eyes still glued to the picture. On the screen, Matthew was at another fashion show, with the hard-faced woman who'd appeared in the opening scene. The camera scanned the catwalk and focused on a young woman, very tall, with wide shoulders and an aristocratic expression.

"That one," Matthew said to the woman next to him. "I'd like that one."

The words "The End" appeared on the screen. People began to clap. To his surprise, Jon found himself clapping too. He was pleased that Fitzgerald had chosen a dark ending. It was more realistic.

"Jon!"

Sarah tugged him after her, into the aisle. Other people were beginning to stand up now, applauding enthusiastically.

"What is it?" Jon asked.

"We've got to get to Brett," Sarah shouted. "I think he's in danger."

"Brett? Why's Brett in danger?"

"I don't know why, but I think that it's Brett he's been after all along. Come on! We've got to warn him!"

Jon was confused. "Who's been after who?" he asked.

But Sarah was already pushing her way down the aisle as the audience began their standing ovation. The picture was a big hit, with this crowd at least.

People tried to congratulate her.

"You were wonderful!"

"You're going to be huge!"

"When you got shot, it was so convincing!"

Sarah ignored them and continued pushing her way through the crowd.

"Where's he sitting?" Jon asked her.

"Over there. At the end of the row."

Jon wished that Sarah had time to explain why Brett was in danger. He could see the actor now. Brett wasn't standing or applauding. But then, you wouldn't, not when you were the star.

"Brett!" Sarah called, but he didn't seem to hear.

A woman was leaning over Brett, telling him how wonderful his performance had been, how he was bound to get an Oscar nomination for it.

"Brett, you've got to get out of here," Sarah said, elbowing aside members of the gathering crowd in order to get to him. Suddenly, the woman talking to Brett became distraught.

"He's been cut. He's been stabbed. Oh, God! There's blood all over him! He's dead!"

Sarah stopped. She turned to Jon. The colour had drained from her face.

"We've got to find Security. They can stop him, if he hasn't escaped already."

Her presence of mind amazed Jon.

"Who?" he asked. "Who did this?"

But Sarah was running over towards one of the

exits. Jon followed her, looking around him. Upstairs, the Royal couple were being ushered out. If there was any risk, they would be the first to be evacuated. Jon guessed that most of the police officers present were with them. He could hear the woman who had found Brett explaining what had happened to anyone who would listen.

"He spoke to me just before the film ended. But, as it finished, this man came over and said something to him. He got really close. I thought that Brett knew him. I thought . . ."

"What did the person look like?"

"It was dark. I couldn't really . . ."

Sarah had found an usher. "Where's Security?" she yelled.

"With the Royals. What's going . . ."

"He's only just got away," Sarah yelled. "The police need to seal the building."

Behind her, there was pandemonium.

"They'll never find him," Sarah said to Jon. "He'll slip away in the confusion."

She turned to the usher. "Did anyone leave as the film was finishing?"

"There was a bloke, yeah, went down the front left exit." The usher pointed at some fire doors a few metres from where they were standing.

"He'll be well gone by now," Jon said.

"Hardly," the usher replied. "All the exits are locked until the Royals are away. We don't want people sneaking in and trying to bump them off."

"In that case . . ." Jon said.

"Come on," Sarah told him. "We're going after him."

"Why?" Jon asked. "Surely it's dangerous? Why can't the police. . .?"

But Sarah was already on her way, hurrying towards the exit on the left of the screen. In the audience, no one was leaving. The manager was standing in front of the screen, appealing for calm.

"Get the police," Jon told the usher. "Tell them we've gone after him."

Jon hurried after Sarah, shouting for her to be careful. By the time she'd pushed her way through the crowd to the exit, he had caught her up.

"He's got a knife," Jon said. "He's dangerous."

"I don't think he'll hurt me," Sarah said. "Not deliberately."

"You still haven't told me who did this," Jon complained. "It's Luke, isn't it?"

Sarah didn't reply. They walked down the corridor marked EXIT. It was a dark, narrow warren, deep beneath the cinema. All of the exit doors led either to this back entrance or to the front of house. Jon and Sarah were nearly at the back door now.

"You still haven't told me who it is," Jon complained again.

"Haven't you worked it out?" Sarah asked him.

"I thought you were the boy detective and I was the unsuspecting girl victim."

"If it isn't Luke," Jon reasoned, "it has to be Leo."

Sarah didn't speak. They turned a corner. The back door was right in front of them. Four different corridors converged here. The killer, Jon knew, was in one of them. In the distance, he could hear doors being opened, people coming. In a moment, the back door would be electronically opened. People would begin spilling out into the West End. If the usher didn't get to the police in time, the killer would be able to merge with the leaving crowd.

Jon looked down each corridor. They were dark, but he couldn't see anyone. Maybe the usher had been wrong. Maybe . . .

"Jon!" Before Jon had time to react to Sarah's warning, someone grabbed him.

"Stay still," a familiar voice said. An arm was locked around Jon's shoulders. He felt a knife being pressed to his throat.

"Let him go," Sarah said, calmly. "You know it won't do any good."

There was blood on the knife: Brett Johnson's blood.

"Give me the knife," Sarah said. "I know you had a reason for what you did. Jon and I will help you explain it."

"Please," Jon said.

Shivering in the dark passageway, Sarah took a step closer to them.

"Give me the knife," she said. "It's over. You got the one you wanted to get. It was only Brett you were after all along, wasn't it?"

"Yes," the boy replied, gruffly. "I never meant to hurt you or the lighting woman." His grip on Jon loosened slightly.

"I thought not," Sarah said calmly. "Tell me what happened."

Slacker took a deep breath. Jon could feel it against his neck.

"The day after the camera plot went wrong, I broke into your room while you were asleep and stole a script. I needed to know where best to get at Brett. First I rigged the engine in the boat, trying to make his death look like an accident. Then I poured extra petrol on the fire at the studio. I knocked Brett out when all the attention was on you. Only he got rescued from the fire and you didn't. Then I persuaded those girls to invade the set on the last day of filming. I switched the guns. But I never meant to hurt you then, either. In the script I had, it was Matthew who got shot."

"I know," Sarah said, holding out her hand for the knife, so that her fingers were only centimetres from Jon's neck. "I worked that out. You saved my life once, didn't you? I'll make sure I tell everybody about that. Please give me the knife now. You're scaring my brother."

For a moment, Jon felt the cold steel brush against his neck. Then it was gone, and Sarah was holding the knife and Slacker was releasing Jon.

"Why?" Sarah asked him. "Why did you do it?"

Slacker spoke shakily, slowly.

"I . . . I had a sister, Emily. She was an actress, got a small part in a film in Hollywood four years ago. Brett Johnson dated her. She wasn't really his girlfriend. She was just a bit of fun for him. He took her for a drive. He'd been drinking, taking drugs. He turned the car over somehow. Emily broke her neck, died instantly. Johnson wasn't hurt at all. He got a suspended sentence." Slacker began to cry.

"She . . . she was twenty-one years old. I was fourteen when it happened. I worshipped her. She had her whole life ahead of her. Emily said that when she made it in the movie business, she'd help me find a job there too. We'd make it together. I miss her so much. She . . . she . . ."

He stopped trying to talk. Sarah dropped the knife on the floor and held him.

"It's all right," she told the boy. "What's your real name?"

"Paul."

"It's all right, Paul. It's all over now."

Jon had stopped shaking now. He watched the boy sobbing in his sister's arms, fixing the image in his mind. He could hear the police coming down one of the corridors and he meant to capture every detail, to hold each one in his memory.

One day, Jon knew, he'd want to make a film about this story, or something like it. He'd want his sister in it too, because she was a good actress and a brave one, as she had just proved. And when he made the film, this would be the final image: the beautiful model in the red dress hugging the long-haired killer in the shabby sports jacket, both of them crying their eyes out.

The audience could work out the rest of the story for themselves from there on.

Cut.

A brand new series coming from Point...

**Encounter worlds where men and women make
hazardous voyages through space; where time
travel is a reality and the fifth dimension a
possibility; where the ultimate horror has
already happened and mankind breaks through
the barrier of technology...**

Obernewtyn
Isobelle Carmody
A new breed of humans are born into a hostile
world struggling back from the brink of
apocalypse...

Random Factor
Jessica Palmer
Battle rages in space. War has been erased from
earth and is now controlled by an all-powerful
computer – until a random factor enters the
system...

First Contact
Nigel Robinson
In 1992 mankind launched the search for extra-
terrestial intelligence. Two hundred years later,
someone responded...

Read Point SF and enter a new dimension...

Point R♥mance

If you like Point Horror, you'll love Point Romance!

Anyone can hear the language of love.

Are you burning with passion, and aching with desire? Then these are the books for you! Point Romance brings you passion, romance, heartache, and most of all, *love . . .*

Saturday Night
Caroline B. Cooney

Summer Dreams, Winter Love
Mary Francis Shura

The Last Great Summer
Carol Stanley

Last Dance
Caroline B. Cooney

Cradle Snatcher
Alison Creaghan

Look out for:

New Year's Eve
Caroline B. Cooney

French Kiss
Robyn Turner

Kiss Me, Stupid
Alison Creaghan

Summer Nights
Caroline B. Cooney

Point R♥mance

Look out for the new Point Romance
mini series coming soon:

First Comes Love
by Jennifer Baker

Can their happiness last?

When eighteen-year-old college junior Julie Miller
elopes with Matt Collins, a wayward and rebellious
biker, no one has high hopes for a happy ending.
They're penniless, cut off from their parents, homeless
and too young. But no one counts on the strength of
their love for one another and
commitment to their vows.
Four novels, *To Have and To Hold, For Better or
Worse, In Sickness and in Health,* and *Till Death Us Do
Part,* follow Matt and Julie through their first
year of marriage.
Once the honeymoon is over, they have to deal with the
realities of life. Money worries, tensions, jealousies,
illness, accidents, and the most heartbreaking decision
of their lives.
Can their love survive?

Four novels to touch your heart...

Point Romance

Caroline B. Cooney

The lives, loves and hopes of five young girls
appear in a dazzling new mini series:

Anne – coming to terms with a terrible secret that
has changed her whole life.

Kip – everyone's best friend, but no one's dream
date...why can't she find the right guy?

Molly – out for revenge against the four girls she
has always been jealous of...

Emily – whose secure and happy life is about to be
threatened by disaster.

Beth Rose – dreaming of love but wondering if it
will ever become a reality.

Follow the five through their last years of high
school, in four brilliant titles: *Saturday Night,
Last Dance, New Year's Eve,* and *Summer Nights*

POINT FANTASY

Read Point Fantasy and escape into the realms of the imagination; the kingdoms of mortal and immortal elements. Lose yourself in the world of the dragon and the dark lord, the princess and the mage; a world where magic rules and the forces of evil are ever poised to attack . . .

Available now:

Doom Sword
Peter Beere
When Adam discovers the Doom Sword he is swept into another kingdom, to face a perilous quest . . .

Brog The Stoop
Joe Boyle
Can Brog restore the Source of Light to Drabwurld, and thus conquer its mortal enemies, the Gork . . .?

The "Renegades" series:
Book 1: Healer's Quest
Book 2: Fire Wars
Jessica Palmer
Meet Zelia, half-human, half-air elemental, and Ares, half-human, half-elf. Journey with them as together they combine their unimaginable powers to battle against evil and restore order to their land . . .

Daine the Hunter:
Book 1: Wild Magic
Book 2: Wolf Speaker
Tamora Pierce
Follow the adventures of the unique and
gifted young heroine, Daine, who is possessed
of a strange and incredible "wild magic" . . .

Foiling the Dragon
Susan Price
What will become of Paul Welsh, pub poet,
when he meets a dragon – with a passion for
poetry, and an appetite for poets . . .

Dragonsbane
Patricia C. Wrede
Princess Cimorene discovers that living with a
dragon is not always easy, and there is a
serious threat at hand . . .